Merie Vision Publishing
Merievisionpublishing@gmail.com

Copyright © 2025 by Jeremy Jae Jae Davis
Uptown Classic Productions

ISBN: 978-1-961213-18-0

Library of Congress control number on record

This is a work of fiction. Names, characters, places, and incidents either are the product of the author's imagination or are used fictitiously. Any resemblance to actual persons, living or dead, events, or locales is entirely coincidental.

All rights reserved. No part of this book may be reproduced in any form either by electronic or mechanical means, including information storage and retrieval systems, without written permission from the publisher, except by a reviewer who may quote brief passages in a review.

Formatting, Editing, and Design by
Merie Vision Publishing, LLC

Front Cover by Che'Von

First Print Edition: July 2025

Printed in the United States of America

My Testimony
BIDDY BOI VS JAE JAE

Jeremy Jae Jae Davis

Introduction...

Have you ever sat down and had an amazing conversation with someone...reminiscing...and afterward said, *"I could write a book about my life?"* I think we all have. Well, I've had plenty of those conversations throughout the years, and guess what? I just so happen to be an author. So, I decided to write a book of short, collective stories from past and present events. Each one has played a major role in shaping my personal growth and journey. These stories not only prepared me, but they built me mentally, physically, and spiritually into the man I am today.

We all have a past. I've just learned to accept mine with a renewed mindset. With that growth, I'm now able to live in my truth and express it freely, without shame or denial. To be honest, when I reflect back on a lot of these short stories, I find them quite entertaining because, once you've grown mentally, you can look back at your past and say, *"Damn, what the hell was I thinking?"* I always tell people, "For anything to grow, disruption has to run its course." Not just my words. It's the law of the universe.

A rose seed in a bag is just a seed in a bag until it's placed in the ground and nurtured by the soil, sun, and rain. Eventually, disruption begins its course, roots begin to form, and in due time, if the season of growth is good, a beautiful rose will emerge from the dirt. I've always compared that nurtured rose to life itself. However you look at it, there's no progression in life without disruption.

Period.

It's never a free ride to success. No matter how you got there, we all must face adversity at some point in our journey. For some people, it'll take more seasons of growth than others, but we *will* all go through disruptive seasons. Just because things didn't work out this season, doesn't mean the next one isn't abundantly yours to claim or manifest.

I always talk about the chaos in the world and that it must exist…just like disruption. However, with a positive mindset, we can all navigate the journey a little more smoothly. When your mindset has been renewed, you start to analyze and make sound decisions, especially when you recognize chaos. Not only is your mind programmed to rethink, but also to *see differently*. With that gift, you'll have the power to impact a bag full of seeds that will one day become beautiful rose gardens that are magnifying and beautifying the earth. Only by renewing their mindsets will they ever realize they are more than just seeds. They are GOD's beautifully designed creation.

I am that rose in the concrete…grown through disruption from having a renewed mindset. I believe God is not finished with me yet. I'm here to serve my purpose and to spread love, joy, and light to the masses through this amazing craft.

Thank you all for your love and support. This is yet another Uptown Classic and Merie Vision Publication for your book collection.

Some of the names, dates, and events may have been changed or altered, but the storylines are based on a true story. This book is for educational and entertainment purposes only

My Testimony...

I grew up in Norfolk, VA, in the early eighties. My mother, Brenda, was a vibrant, hard-working, loving woman. At the tender age of twenty-four, she raised three children. My mother worked as a housekeeper at the Scottish Inn motel, just off Military Highway. It was there that she worked countless hours to make sure we had everything we would ask her for.

My sister, Christiana Nixon, aka "Pooh-Pooh," was the eldest. My brother, Toronto "Tee-Tee" Davis, was the middle child, with me being the youngest. My mother had actually given birth to another baby boy, but he died of crib death before I was born. His name was Jermaine Davis. My mother said I came out looking exactly like him. I never remembered my father. He'd gotten incarcerated while I was an infant. So growing up, I would hear stories of him being this ruthless street hustler. Later on in my life, I would bump into a few old-head convicts who did time with him, and they would tell me penitentiary stories of how he made some of the best prison hooch.

Growing up an adolescent, I would often aggravate my siblings, and in return, they would tease me by saying, "That's why your daddy's a jailbird." To be honest, that used to crush my little heart, but I wouldn't allow them to know it. My sister was good at making that statement a part of her daily vocabulary. Her father's name was Larry, and he was a deadbeat but would pop up every so often just to show his face. My sister loved her some *Larrrry*. I don't recall ever saying two words to him. For some reason, he looked awfully strange to me with his greasy slick-back hair, big protruding eyeballs, and enormous lips. He actually looked half man, half catfish. Lol. Sorry, sis, but my get-back has been long-awaited and well anticipated. My brother Toronto's father's name was Herbert. His name rang bells throughout the city of Norfolk for putting in work on the streets.

One day, I recall my brother telling me that he had more siblings, including a set of twin brothers and a few sisters. His father, Herbert, was without a doubt a rolling stone.

Fortunately, through God's amazing grace and mercy, my mother had help raising me. Even though my father was incarcerated, that didn't make one bit of a difference. Since I can remember, I've always been an Etheridge. My late grandmother, Odessa Lee Etheridge, the matriarch of the family, was born and raised in Elizabeth City, NC. She moved to Norfolk, VA in the sixties. There, she gave birth to ten children. Starting with the eldest was my mother/aunt Elvira, my uncle Darry aka "Funk," Bobby aka "Rob," and my late uncle Keith, who passed away before I was born. I was told he drowned in a lake. My Uncle Wilson, aka "Weo," was incarcerated for most of my upbringing. Dwight was, and still to this day, a father figure. Leroy, aka "Curtis," was the youngest of them all, and I looked up to him like a big brother, along with my father, Michael, and both his sisters, my aunts Joyce and Angela.

My mother's side of the family was small. My late grandmother, Christine Nixon, gave birth to six children, with my mother, Brenda, being the eldest. Uncle Billy moved to Detroit when I was a baby, and we never heard from him again. To be honest, I thought he was dead. Would you believe that forty years later, he showed up at my mother's doorstep smiling and wanting hugs and shit? Everyone was in shock and calling each other's phones like, "Guess who popped up out of his grave?" Of course, my mother embraced him with love because that's just the kind of loving person she is. Not me, though. I needed to hear a valid reason as to why he abandoned his family. So much had happened in the past forty years. He even missed his mother's and sister's funerals. I wasn't trying to hear nothing other than he had been incarcerated on death row and President

Biden had released him on a pardon, or somehow he'd struck it rich and had finally come home to spread the wealth. Forty years was a long time to be away from your family when you're able to see them. I still feel some type of way about my Uncle Billy's situation after finding out he wasn't incarcerated or hadn't struck it rich. He could have stayed his Black ass in Detroit for all I care, and that's just what it is.

My late aunt "Time Bomb" was a dark-skinned, beautiful woman and could burn in that kitchen. Her food was amazing. I can still taste her collards and mac n' cheese. She was indeed a cooking woman. I miss her so much. My uncle Pennyman was incarcerated for most of my life. His baby sister, my aunt "Boo-Boo," is one of my favorite aunts. As adults, we became best friends. I recall many days smoking weed with her while laughing our hearts out. I never realized how funny I actually was until then. My uncle Chris was the uncle in the family who always went to jail. Growing up, whenever he came home, we would all rush to go and see him because, more than likely, he would be going back soon. We grew up knowing that prison was Uncle Chris' real home, and our world was just a vacation for him.

I can recall all the way back to Lafayette Shores, where I vividly remember living in a blue bungalow. My two aunts, Boo-Boo and Pracilla, also lived in the neighborhood. We lived in the projects, but the love was rich. I recall bouncing from house to house on any given day. Both of my aunts' houses felt like home. I played, slept, and ate there often. My aunt Pracilla had two boys, Antonio Nixon and Corey "Lil Meek" Nixon. My aunt Boo-Boo had one child, Lewis aka "Binky."

In 1985, my mother began dating Warren, aka "Jake." He was a beach-cruiser-riding, weed-selling, woman-beating, alcoholic, fake azz Rastafarian. I recall him not having a job. He sat in the house all day listening to Bob Marley while bagging up weed. This man would often beat on my mother in front of us. If I ever hated an individual, he would be the first. I couldn't wait until I got older so I could kick his ass. That day would soon manifest, but that's later on in my story.

Back 'N the Days…

I can recall the summer of 1987 like it was yesterday. It seemed like everybody and their momma was blasting LL Cool J's *"I Need Love"* or *"I'm Bad,"* Kool Moe Dee's *"Wild, Wild West,"* or that new hit single *"Top Billin'"* by Audio Two. Whether it was in cars, Walkmans, home stereos, or boom boxes, you heard it *everywhere*.

That summer, my mother finally had enough. She decided she was leaving Jake. So, we moved from Lafayette Shores to Park Place. Her best friend, Miss Loretta, was a sweetheart. I can't recall one time she was ever mean to me or my siblings, so I was overjoyed that we'd be staying with her. Miss Loretta lived in a downstairs, four-bedroom, two-and-a-half-bath apartment on 35th Street. She invited my mother to live with her until she could get back on her feet. From what I remember, Miss Loretta never liked that fake Rastafarian at all. I was elated. That meant he wouldn't be coming around my mama anymore.

Park Place was fun. To make it even better, we lived just two blocks away from the legendary City Park. That's where I started spending countless hours on the basketball courts, perfecting my skills. After shooting around, I'd walk across the street to the zoo to see my favorite spider monkeys. They made this loud, annoying whooping sound you could hear from blocks away. If you mimicked them, they'd sometimes get irritated and start tossing feces at you. No lie. I had a few close calls messing with those damn monkeys. Miss Loretta had moved to Virginia from Memphis, Tennessee. She and her kids, Hawk and Kandy, had that deep Southern drawl, but I could tell right away they were spoiled.

Hawk had a Nintendo before I even knew what it was. He had all the exclusive games such as *RBI Baseball*, *Tecmo Bowl*, *Street Fighter*, and *Mario Bros*. Hawk was around the same age as my sister and brother, so I had to get in where I fit in...usually when they were sleeping or outside. Kandy was more my age, but she only had girl toys. Even back then, I knew it didn't feel masculine to play with Barbie and Ken dolls. So, I'd always suggest we play "house," and I would tell her to hurry up and feed the dolls and put them to bed... so we could get to the *good part*. That felt better than playing *Mario Bros* any day. Our parents used to say we were cousins, but even back then, we knew that was far from the truth. All seven of us lived in that apartment stress-free for the whole year. It was one of the best times I can remember. You know, when you're having fun, time always seems to fly by.

I remember Wanda Pooh, who later passed, her sister Peaches, and her brother Nick. They lived directly across the street from us, and we'd all grow up together for years to come. We had fun just walking the neighborhood and boldly trespassing in people's backyards. Nick wasn't scared of heights, so he was our designated climber. He could scale a pecan, apple, or peach tree effortlessly and shake the branches until everything hit the ground. Sometimes we'd run into an old grumpy person yelling at us to get the hell out of their yard. Most of the time, they didn't mind as long as we ate the fruit and didn't litter their yard from our regular fruit fights.

By 1988, Bobby Brown's *"Don't Be Cruel"* blasted through my mother's home stereo. We had moved out of Miss Loretta's and into our own apartment on 29th Street and Llewellyn. I couldn't have been happier to have my own space. At first, my brother Tee-Tee and I shared the bed and the room, but eventually, we got a bunk bed set with matching dressers from my mother's favorite furniture store, Meyers & Tabakin. It felt good to finally have my *own* bed and live in our *own* house.

My late grandfather, Bobby Barfield, lived on 34th Street. He was raising my three cousins, Tasha, Lisa, and Shavon. This was after their mother, my Aunt Wanda Barfield, was killed by her boyfriend. Grandaddy's house was official. He had cable, a VCR, a house phone, and he'd pack us into one of his many Cadillacs and drive us all through Norfolk sightseeing. It felt like everybody in every neighborhood knew him. We had so much fun at Grandaddy's house that my siblings and I started walking from 29th to 34th Street every day. He made the best oatmeal, which he called *hot cereal*. He'd add raisins, milk, butter, cinnamon, and brown sugar. It tasted absolutely amazing, and he made it in this gigantic pot. I've never had oatmeal that good since. I could eat several bowls in one sitting, and all he'd say was, "Eat up, grandson, it's good for you." He also went to the local dairy to buy buckets of ice cream and served it on cones all summer long. He was the first person to take me fishing, too. I wasn't big on touching worms, but I'll always be grateful for the experience.

Whenever my mother got her food stamps, she'd let us pick out whatever items we wanted. Of course, I wanted oatmeal, cereal, cookies, and ice cream...Grandaddy did that to me, but we always had to wait until we left Murray's Steakhouse first. They had all the discounts – buy two bags of party wings, get another free. Same with their chicken nuggets and strips. You already know that my mom stocked up on that barnyard pimp. She was always a cool mom.

By 1991, I was twelve. I remember being heavily influenced by Kris Kross. I started wearing my baseball jersey and Guess jeans backward to school. At the time, it just seemed like the cool thing to do. I guess I was finding my identity. My mom didn't trip, but my Aunt Elvira?.. Now *that's* another story.

Aunt Elvira

Aunt Elvira has always been nothing less than a loving and caring mother to me. Our story dates back to one spring evening in 1979 when my father, Michael, arrived at my grandmother's doorstep with me wrapped up in a cardboard box stuffed with toys. I don't know what was up with the cardboard box, but the story goes that I was a little over six months old. My Aunt Elvira said I was so tiny, and I didn't cry at all. She told me she remembered me holding onto her tightly, as if I didn't want to be dropped.

Growing up, I heard stories from family members...even my older sister once or twice...saying they thought my Aunt Elvira was a mean person. That's something I personally couldn't relate to, even if I tried. My aunt was unique in her own way, but to know her was to love her. So, if anyone ever thought of her as mean, they clearly didn't have a clue how much of a beautiful soul she actually was. In return, my siblings would say, "That's because she loves you like you're her own." That, I have to agree, was nothing but the absolute truth.

To my knowledge, my Aunt Elvira never biologically had a child of her own, but I've always looked at her as my mother, and she's always looked at me as her son. She helped my mother raise me ever since the day I arrived with my father. She just recently revealed to me that my mother named me Jeremy, and that she nicknamed me Jae-Jae because she never liked the name "Biddy Boi" that her siblings used to call me. She told me "Biddy Boi," to her, meant defenseless and helpless, so she never called me that. While writing this, I called my mother intending to hear the complete opposite, but she confirmed that my Aunt Elvira did, in fact, nickname me. I'm just discovering this newfound information about myself in my mid-forties. Even though I wish I'd known it earlier, I'm grateful they were both open and transparent.

    My Aunt Elvira loved and cared for me deeply, and not only did I know it, but I felt it. I bonded with her, and never once have I looked at her any differently than I did my own birth mother. I had everything I needed, and most of the time, everything I wanted. Christmas was always an epic event, and birthdays were amazing. I can recall having plenty of food, a gigantic birthday cake, and lots of new clothes, bookbags, and school supplies. My birthday would always land on or around Labor Day, which meant school would be starting the following Monday.

    Summer at Grandma's house was always fun. I would return to Park Place, where my sister and brother were, and I couldn't wait to show out with all the new toys, clothes, and shoes my jailbird daddy's sister had brought me. I say my grandmother's, but it was actually my Aunt Elvira's house. It was there I was taught manners such as washing your hands before opening the refrigerator, saying grace before every meal, and always saying "please" and "thank you." After eating dinner, I learned to excuse myself from the table before leaving. I also learned how to wash dishes and cut grass. Cutting grass was always fun because Aunt Elvira had bought a riding mower. To a twelve-year-old, that was nothing but a fun-filled day.

We often went to church on Sundays. New Rising Sun Baptist Church sat at the foot of the Berkley Bridge. Reverend Zack Pippens Jr. and Pastor Marcellus Scott preached the Word. I remember being excited to go to church just so I could watch Cecile play the drums. He was this five-foot midget of a man, but boy was he a giant on those drums. Miss Lisa and her sister Jackie were two soulful singing sisters. I could never forget them. I just couldn't wait until church was finally over so I could hop on Cecil's drum set and make a bunch of unnecessary noise.

My late grandmother, Odessa Lee Etheridge, would always make me sit beside her the entire service. I can still recall the church being hotter than holy hell. The blazing temperature often made me doze off, but my grandmother would always catch me right before I fell into a deep coma. She'd gently pop me on my head, grab a fan, and start fanning me. Then, she'd stuff my mouth with one of those stale peppermints from the bottom of her purse. I was going to get that *Word* in me if Odessa had anything to do with it. One of her favorite songs was *Prayed for Me*, and forty-something years later, I still remember it word for word.

My Aunt Elvira and Uncle Dwight both held key positions in the church and were highly respected, from what I observed. I can honestly say I grew up in the church, and even though most of the time I was ready to leave, I definitely learned knowledge, wisdom, and understanding of the Word. It still resonates with me today and has helped carry me through some of my darkest moments. Thank you, Grandma, for keeping me awake in church and making sure I received the anointing. I just recently lost my grandmother while writing this book, and no amount of words can ever express how I truly feel. I'm taking this time to reflect on the great woman she was and the unlimited love she blessed generations with. I believe in my heart that I was the closest to my grandmother out of all her grandchildren, great-grandchildren, and great-great-grandchildren. She played a pivotal role in my upbringing as her first grandson.

Man, she made the best dumplings ever...along with her secret sweet potato pie recipe. I can still picture Thanksgiving and Christmas Eve, with her playing the Temptations' Christmas album while baking pies, and all my aunties and uncles rushing to get their own pie. That's how good they were.

I will forever love you, Grandma. Thank you for always loving me unconditionally.

This book is dedicated to you, Odessa.

Uncle Dwight

He called me "Biddy." As a matter of fact, he remixed an old seventies song by Martha and the Vandellas called *Jimmy Mack* and began singing his own rendition, *Biddy Mack*. I recall laughing my little heart out whenever he'd hit this certain high note. He was, and has always been, the father figure I needed in my life. I'm so thankful and blessed to have him. Still to this day, he's just a call or text away. As far back as I can remember, he's always been special to me. He once told me that he and his siblings would form a circle around me and all yell "Biddy Boi!!" at the same time just to see who I would crawl toward. From what I've been told, I'd look around first, spot my uncle Dwight, and crawl straight to him every single time. I think that's where our bond began.

My other uncles had love for me, but man, Uncle Dwight's love hit different. He *demonstrated* his love and affection. Still to this day, I hate disappointing him because I know how much he truly loves and believes in me. I would always tell people that he's never verbally told me "no" about anything. If he wasn't able to do something, no matter what it was, he would say, "Nephew, let Unk get back with you." To be totally honest, I've probably heard that once, maybe twice, in my whole life. I told you. I was spoiled. My uncle Dwight Alexander Etheridge Sr. is a gem. They don't breed them like him anymore.

    He is and will always be my superhero. He taught me things my mother and Aunt Elvira couldn't. I recall getting put on punishment all the time for peeing in my pants. I can still see the frustration on my mother's face.

    "At seven years old, you shouldn't be Pissy Paul," she would always say.

    I didn't understand. I would go to the bathroom whenever I had to, but for some reason I'd still leak into my undies every time. I did it so much, I started to think it was normal until one evening, Uncle Dwight took me to an event. I remember we went to the restroom together. He stood at the big urinal, and I stood at the small one. I mimicked everything he did because I wanted to be just like him. After he finished peeing, he began to shake. I'd never seen that done before, but I tried it. Lo and behold, the minute I put my worm back in my pants, there was absolutely no leaking. I was elated. My mother eventually noticed my undies were dry and stopped calling me "Pissy Paul." She never knew the real reason was because I had a man in my life who could teach me things she or Aunt Elvira just couldn't. So, when people say a woman can't teach a boy how to be a man, it's true. Just like a man can't teach a girl how to be a woman. From my experience, I'm a firm believer.

    Growing up, Uncle Dwight was my example of what a real man was. He loved his wife Joyce, and my God, she loved and adored him right back. She had this twinkle in her eye whenever she said his name. It was one of the prettiest Colgate smiles you could imagine. I always wanted my future wife to feel that same way when she said *my* name. Uncle Dwight presented me with countless business opportunities out of love because let's be real, my résumé didn't qualify me for some of the positions he gave me. He was the owner and CEO of Geniuses Staffing, a temp service. He gave me job after job, after job. Even when I fumbled the rock, he'd just have Gary fire me, but somehow, a few months later, he'd find me and say, "Show up at the office ready for work." I learned a lot of computer and business administration skills working at Geniuses Staffing. Now, I'm looking forward to rebuilding my bond with my uncle. The moment we're face to face, he'll see. He has no clue of the man I've grown to be, but that's later in my story…

My Uncle Curtis

He called me "Biddy Boi." He was more like a big brother to me. Curt also demonstrated his love. I just remember always having fun with him. He was funny, and he loved to travel. I admired the competitive spirit he had on the basketball court. He never really got the opportunity to see me in rare form and dominating the blacktop everywhere I played. I feel like he saw the talent in me early on because he would always come to pick me up to go to the gym. He also bought me my very first official car. It was a sky blue 1988 Nissan Maxima with eighteen-inch chrome rims. I remember the day he bought it from the auction. He told me to drive it straight home and park it. It wasn't registered yet, and I didn't have my license, but he'd already signed me up for driving school. Being the hardheaded adolescent I was, I drove home as instructed…

just not *directly*. I stopped at the Ace Hardware store and made a copy of the key.

    Curt showed up a couple of hours later asking for the keys. Of course, I handed them over quickly, but as soon as he drove off, I was back in the driver's seat within minutes, bumping "Money, Cash, Hoes" by Jay-Z featuring DMX. That ungratefulness would soon come back my way tenfold. I had the *worst* luck with that car. I now understand, through knowledge, wisdom, understanding, and the universal laws of attraction, why those things happened. I regret a lot of things I've done, and people I've hurt and disappointed. If I could go back and fix them, I would, but life doesn't work like that. All I can do now is allow my renewed thinking and growth to speak volumes for me. I'm also looking forward to rebuilding my bond with Uncle Curtis. He still has that dog in him, but I think I'll crush him on the blacktop. We'll just have to see when that day comes.

My Sister Christine
    Onyx's newest banger "Slam" blasted through my brand-new yellow Sony Walkman, along with my top-of-the-line earbuds that my jailbird daddy's sister bought for me. My sister started hating again, like always. She reached over, tapped me on my shoulder, and yelled at the top of her lungs for me to turn them down or go outside because she was trying to watch *Purple Rain* for the thousandth time. I decided to exit stage left. With her, there were no wins. So, I went upstairs to my bedroom. I never understood her obsession with a four-foot-eleven man who wore high heels and makeup. I guess I'd just sit in the window and watch the neighborhood kids play. I didn't know anybody from Uptown. We were the new kids on the

block, and to be honest, I really wasn't feeling the park vibe.

At least out in Park Place, I could walk over to City Park and play a couple of pickup basketball games, or visit the Norfolk Zoo next door and mess around with the spider monkeys throwing poop. I know it sounds crazy, but it gave me an adrenaline rush knowing that they knew *exactly* what they were doing. I swear, one time a monkey faked like he was throwing poop at me, and I ducked and started running. I happened to look back and caught him actually laughing his heart out at me. After that day, it was on. Monkeys are smarter than people think, especially those ratchet ones at the Norfolk Zoo. Even if I got tired of running from flying monkey poop, I could walk a few blocks down to the Colonial Boys & Girls Club, I could walk over to Miss Loretta's house and play Nintendo with Hawk, or I would even play "house" with his sister, Kandy. I could never go wrong with that. I loved the fact that I had options.

I could even walk two blocks and make a pit stop on 34th Street at my granddaddy's. Nine times out of ten, he was already out driving somewhere in his Buick Regal or one of his clean Cadillac Broughams. My granddaddy kept official cars back in the day. I never really noticed that about him until I got older. I guess that's where my love for automobiles came from. One thing about Bobby, he always enjoyed my company and was always down for a ride-along with me. Even if I showed up and he'd already left, my three cousins, Tasha, Shavon, and Lisa, would likely have some of their friends over playing hopscotch or double-dutch. Most of their friends I knew from Stuart Elementary School. I've always been a well-dressed, popular individual.

You see, Park Place allowed me to be a kid, but when we moved Uptown, I began to lose my innocence.

Before I could even realize what was happening, I'd already become a product of my environment. All my peers were selling drugs and doing grown-up things that I had no clue how to do. They'd all stand on the block with the older posse and smoke Newport shorts and Philly blunts. Some were shooting dice, and others were rapping in cyphers while selling drugs to the local dope fiends. It didn't take long for me to realize that Uptown moved way faster than Park Place and the kids my age couldn't care less about Nintendo, the zoo, City Park, or humping around on girls our age. I knew, if I wanted to fit in, I had to get in tune with what was happening or stick out like a sore thumb.

Overall, what I *did* know was, I wasn't going to be hustling on nobody's street corner. I'd seen it too many times how the cops jumped out and harassed the crew, and some even went to jail. There was something in me that looked past the fear and the consequences of my decisions. I didn't know or care how I was going to get it. I just knew in my heart that I was going to get myself some money.

My sister started dating some of the most well-known, money-getting dope boys Uptown. I couldn't believe my mother even approved of it. Then again, she dated a weed-selling, abusive, beach-cruiser-riding, fake Rastafarian ninja. So, I guess my sister got it honest. If I can be totally real, I'd have to admit I was blown away seeing this drug dealer pull up to our house blasting the classic Lost Boyz song "Renee" in his cocaine-white, red-leather interior 300E Mercedes-Benz, sitting on eighteen-inch all-white custom Ashanti rims. He stepped out of the car wearing a pair of gold Cartier frames and a five-inch herringbone necklace that sat on top of his Coogi sweater. He had a presidential plain Jane, limited-edition Rolex watch on his right arm, along with a chunky princess-cut diamond bracelet and pinky ring on his left hand. This was in the mid-nineties because the money and the drugs were *plentiful.*

Mannn!! You couldn't tell me he wasn't the sweetest nucca in the hood. When my sister looked up and saw him walking into our house, she folded like a paper napkin. From what I observed, he was cool, generous, and respectful toward my sister and mother. Every time he came around, he brought gifts and hundred-dollar bills for everybody. It was at that very moment that I realized money didn't just make *me* happy, it made the people around me just as happy. That was another reason I wanted to be nothing less than an official dope boi.

I was just listening to Nas rap about that same car he'd just parked in front of our house in his self-titled song "Street Dreams." It felt like he was sent to me by the Dope Boi Gods. Even though I knew it wasn't right, I was intrigued by everything about him. I knew in my heart that I could be just as rich as him, if not richer, but I also understood I had to hustle just as hard.

My Brother Tee-Tee

We grew up together, but by the time I turned seventeen, he was incarcerated. My mother was devastated. I still recall the morning that the detectives came to our house and told her they had him in custody. My brother was charged with multiple robberies along with several others. I knew my brother and his friends weren't angels by far, but multiple robberies just didn't sound like something they'd be into.

Allegedly, my brother Tee-Tee, was the getaway driver. His defense was that he never left the vehicle, so he didn't have a clue about the robberies that were taking place. I knew my brother like the back of my hand, and he was too damn scary to rob anybody. He didn't deserve to be in jail or prison for the amount of time the prosecution was talking about. I hated seeing my mother cry... that shit did something to me. Not hearing her talk for weeks was devastating. I couldn't take it any longer, and I had to do something to help my mother and brother. That summer, I had already jumped off the porch and started hustling a little weed and crack here and there just to maintain my personal lifestyle. My sister's new boyfriend was rich as hell and was now my connect. He was cool, but a little scary at times. I respected how he moved... better safe than sorry.

    It was starting to look bad for my brother. I was told Peter Decker was the best defense attorney in Norfolk. So, for the next three months, day in and day out, I stayed on the block hustling to get his retainer fee. Peter Decker wanted twenty thousand dollars, with a ten-thousand-dollar deposit. He said my brother would, more than likely, still do a minimum of five years in the Virginia Department of Corrections... *if* he took the case. Talk about robbery without a gun. That should be a crime in itself, but I was determined to get the money, so I went extra hard on the block at night.

    During the day, I hustled out of the infamous Town Point Motel. That's where I began to run my bag up. There was no such thing as sleep for me, just cat naps. When I say that motel jumped all day and night, I haven't seen anything like it since the Carter in *New Jack City*. There wasn't anything you wanted or needed that wasn't available at that motel. I averaged at least thirty-five hundred in a matter of hours, every day... not including what I made at night on my block.

    They say a determined mind is like a train with no brakes... well, literally, that was me. I hustled so hard my connect stopped answering his phone. I was like, *for real yo'?* At a time when I really needed that work. After I calmed down and got myself together, I smoked a blunt and counted my profit. That's when I realized I hadn't brushed my teeth or washed my ass in days. My waves had turned into a mini afro, and I was losing weight I couldn't afford to lose from just smoking weed and not eating. I was already skinny. People I knew started seeing me leaving Town Point regularly and assumed I was getting high... but never that. I was getting money.

    I understand now why my old connect didn't answer his phone. Imagine going from copping four and a baby to a half bird in a matter of weeks. In his mind, there was no way possible that an eighteen-year-old was hustling that hard and doing numbers at that astronomical rate... unless he wasn't spending any money. At that time, he couldn't see my flamboyant, pretty boy ass pulling that off. Only if he knew…I only spent money on snacks, gas, my motel room, and…okay, I may have tricked a little bit, but that was it. I spent my weed sales on all of that, so there was no way he could calculate my bread.

    Through it all, I kept a low profile. I couldn't afford the risk of getting caught. What use would I be with both of us in jail? All the money I made would've gone to another lawyer, commissary, and the phone. My most disappointing moment came when I was told the retainer fee went up to twenty-five thousand dollars. Mr. Decker said the fee increased because my brother's preliminary hearing had already been certified to the high courts for jury selection.

    Mr. Decker saw the frustration in my face and said, "With a jury trial, he's going to get convicted. I've personally gone over his case. My investigators talked to the detective, we interviewed several witnesses for the state, and they've all been subpoenaed to testify against your brother. His co-defendants have all taken plea deals." He looked me dead in my eyes and said, "Save your money," before handing me back my second retainer. "I don't want it if I can't get him a reasonable sentence."

That's when I knew my brother was duct tape.

Now, I had enough money to get me some real weight, so it was on. I hustled out of determination, pain, adversity, and ambition. There was no way anybody Uptown was going to out-hustle me. I purchased my first bird from a new connect for a reasonable price. I remember taking it back to my room and staring at it like it was a newborn baby. My homeboy was with me at the time and said his auntie could stretch it to a bird and a half…if the coke was good enough. I told him I had it all on the line and couldn't afford any mishaps. He agreed, and we left the hood with a few samples. Albo snorted a line, and his nose started bleeding. He looked up at me and said, "You got yourself a missile, nephew."

I watched Kim stir and mix the coke and baking soda like she was making homemade soup. She told us to grab the ice, and when she sat it on top, all I heard was crackling noises. Kim had just stretched my brick to a brick and a half. I ended up selling the half bird that same day for what I paid for the whole brick. Me and my ace and sat and bagged and tagged eight balls, quarters, and breakdown packages all night. It was all profit from here and the beginning of a Dope Boi on the rise.

Young's Park

My mother moved there in 1993. When I turned eighteen, I had several sets of Park House keys. The Norfolk Redevelopment and Housing Authority was placing young mothers in small or big units, depending on how many children were on their lease. Their rent was based on income. They didn't pay for water or electricity, just a set rent, and they couldn't have a man or boyfriend living with them in the unit, or they would get evicted. Growing up, I'd heard horror stories of young girls getting evicted for not being able to pay fifty dollars in rent. Maybe if they had a man in the house, that wouldn't have happened.

    I paid several females' rent regularly just to use their unit. Whenever you're hustling out the hood, the more units you have access to when the shit hits the fan, the better. Plus, I always liked to be ducked off. I even had a white girl who lived on the outskirts of the hood. I caught her at the local Shop-N-Go. She kept side-eyeing me, so I approached her. After finding out she occupied a unit, I gave her a business proposition. Two days later, I moved my safe into her spot. My drugs were in another unit. My clothes and guns were in others. Okay, so I chose the snow bunny to hold my cash…don't judge me.

    Growing up, a lot of young Black women looked forward to having their own Park House when they turned eighteen, instead of living in the real world and paying bills. I believe it's a trap for women and their children, but if you can benefit and move forward, then you beat the odds. My mother, unfortunately, didn't beat the odds. She got complacent and comfortable for decades. To this day, she's still there. She had so many opportunities to move, but she always refused. She would always say that if she moved, she'd be miserable and die.

    My mother is the true definition of a Park Girl. I remember it was a cold winter evening. I had just left one of my units. I had no plans on visiting my mother, but for some reason, I decided to make a pit stop. I never knocked unless the door was locked. In this case, I turned the knob and walked right in. My sister, Christina, had this disturbed look on her face. I'd seen that face a time or two, and I knew something wasn't right.

"Where's Ma?" I asked.

Before she could say anything, my mother came out trying to downplay what Jake had just done, saying he shoved her into the refrigerator and that she told him to get the hell out. I was looking at my sister's face the entire time my mother was talking. Without her saying one word, her expression was telling me my mom was lying. This was the moment I'd been waiting for. Jake had been getting away with putting his hands on my mother for decades. I couldn't believe this fool stayed around long enough for me to get big enough to kick his ass. I acted as if everything was okay and left. I knew he was at work, but he would usually be riding his dumb-ass beach cruiser through the field around five-thirty. He hadn't seen me in a while. Most of the time when I visited my mom, he was at work. Plus, he thought I had moved to North Carolina months ago with this chick I was dating, who his sister knew.

The plan was set. Catch him outside, or my mom would take up for him.

So, me and my crew laid on Jake until we spotted him riding through the field, just like I said he would, hard hat on, drinking a forty-ounce, and clueless as hell about what was about to happen to him. We jumped out and surprised him. My homie pushed him off his bike, and we stomped him out. He balled up in a knot and lay there. My other homie pulled out this long blade and began cutting Jake's dreadlocks. I had my gun on me. I pointed it at him and told him to stand up. He stood up. I pressed the gun into his forehead, gritting my teeth. He began begging and pleading for his life.

"Please, Jae-Jae... don't do this."

All I heard was my homie whisper, "KILL his azz!"

Jake's eyeballs almost flew out of his head. Luckily for him, I wasn't a follower. I told him to get his shit out of my mother's house and never come back. If he ever showed his face again, I was going to kill him. I decided not to even go past my mother's house for a week or two. I didn't want to hear her hollering and screaming, "Why would you do that to him?" or the "I already raised my children, let me love who I love," speech again.

See, I'd beaten Jake's ass before, and I had to hear that. So, I could only imagine what she was going to say when his telling-ass told her I put a gun to his head. I entered my mother's house as usual, without knocking. She and my sister were both sitting at the table watching a movie while eating.

She looked up and asked, "Jae-Jae, have you seen Jake?"

I looked back at her, confused, and replied, "Hey, to you too, Ma."

She said Jake had been missing for two weeks. She said the last time she saw him, he rushed into the house and packed his bags without saying a word. He was in and out in a matter of minutes. I looked at my mother and shrugged my shoulders like I had a clue in the world, but when I looked over at my sister, it was like she knew the count.

Five years later, my mom ran into Jake at his mother's funeral. He described to her in detail what happened to him that winter evening. He told her I was a lunatic, that he was scared for his life, and that's the reason he never returned. To be honest, I'm glad he didn't because, as Allah is my witness, I meant what I said. I know he knew it too.

My mom wasn't even mad about it. I mean... it was five years of peace and happiness. She was in the healthiest mindset she'd ever been in for years, and it felt absolutely amazing to hear her say, "Thank you for getting rid of him, son."

Even though I barely showed up, my mother knew I was always just a unit away. Jake passed away years ago, but what he did to my mental health left a stain on me. One I would soon recover from, but that's later on in my story.

Adrenaline Junkie...

Back in Chesapeake, my Aunt Elvira was not having me walking around with my pants sagging or talking with a whole lot of slang. Things were different at my grandmother's house. It was quiet, peaceful, and I had everything a kid my age could ask for. I enjoyed getting away from Norfolk and all the chaos that surrounded my life daily. I knew my aunts and uncles didn't have a clue about the magnitude of arson I was committing, or had been involved in, back home. Whenever I came over to my grandmother's house, I felt like I was another kid in another body and living in a different world. It was almost as if time stopped, and the world I'd left behind temporarily didn't exist. When all I wanted was to have fun and be Biddy Boi for the weekend, somehow, Jae-Jae would always seem to appear.

Growing up, I didn't want structure. I wanted to be able to do what I wanted to do because, with structure, comes consequences and repercussions. I loved me some Boston baked beans, Little Debbie oatmeal pies, Mr. Goodbars, sunflower seeds, and Now & Laters. Whenever I stole from the corner store, my mother would say, "Jae-Jae, you keep stealing from that store and your ass is going to get caught."

My intention was to prove her wrong by stealing and *not* getting caught, instead of just not stealing and not having to worry about getting caught. Maybe I just had a different way of processing information, but to hell with all of that, it's no excuse. I still knew right from wrong. If I stole while I was at my grandmother's, there were going to be consequences and repercussions *on sight*, and I had a lot of uncles and aunts to answer to. Being a kid growing up in two different homes with different sets of values was very confusing. I never *had* to steal, period. It was just the thrill of taking something and getting away with it. If I *did* get caught, the conniving act of lying my way out of it was the ultimate rush for me.

My Aunt Elvira never once beat me, but her words were sharp as Chinese knives. They would hurt me to my heart, knowing I disappointed her. No kid wants to disappoint the person they know loves and cares for them and would give them the world if they could. After countless hours of medical research, I was able to discover that I suffered from anxiety, depression, and a rare form of child identity crisis. Medical statistics state that 47% of children suffer from an identity crisis, and 67% suffer from bipolar disorder, anxiety, and depression.

That's a high number.

Thirty-four years later, after growth and a renewed, healthy state of mind, Alhamdulillah, I realized how vital mental health is in our community. It's a touchy topic that our people seem to shy away from or just overlook. We all have to admit, growing up, we knew a crazy Tasha or a burnt-out Tony, or maybe even a troubled child named Jae-Jae. My ultimate goal is to dedicate my time and energy to shedding light and education on these high statistics in our community.

My Fire For Fire Trucks

I've always had a love for fire trucks. My grandmother's house was just a few blocks from Fire Station No. 3 in South Norfolk. It was so close, I could stand on the back porch and hit it with a rock. I used to get an adrenaline rush just hearing the loud siren. I was quick to run out the back door just to get a glimpse of the fire truck. Whenever I went back home, I would always hear way more police and ambulance sirens, but to me, there was nothing like a fire truck siren. So, with that being said, I would purposely set fires. Then, I would walk to the nearest telephone booth and dial 911, just so I could watch the fire engine pull in and extinguish it.

Seeing that gave me the ultimate adrenaline rush, knowing that I was the person responsible for all of this. It got to a point where I'd gotten away with setting so many fires that I thought I was invincible. My mother had never gone into my bedroom. She used to always say, "Clean your room before I do. And if you have something you're not supposed to have, I'm going to find it." So, believe it or not, my room stayed super clean.

Norfolk Redevelopment and Housing has yearly inspections. During this particular time, I happened to be staying at my grandmother's house when my mother's inspection arrived. She entered my room and discovered a fire kit under my bed. It was a square box that contained over twenty cigarette lighters and a five-ounce can of lighter fluid. Yeah, I was definitely setting it off way before Jada Pinkett. If I had been a grown man, they would have labeled me a serial arsonist.

In my heart, I think my mom knew I'd been the person responsible for setting the fires all over the projects. One time, I recall I set a fire down the street from our house. I dialed 911, and as soon as I hung up, I turned around and noticed my mother sitting on the porch, watching me. Five minutes later, two fire trucks and an ambulance came flying past our house in the direction of the fire. I realize now how dangerous setting those fires was, and I'm so grateful nobody was ever hurt due to my ignorance.

When I lived out in Park Place, there was so much I could do as a kid, even if it was dodging monkey poop, climbing fruit trees, or attending the Colonial Boys & Girls Club. Whenever you take a child from one environment into another, it is indeed a culture shock. Even though living uptown forced me to grow up fast, there was still a lot of *kid* in me. As an adult, I look back at a lot of the things I did as a troubled youth, and I can't believe I'm still here to be able to tell these stories. The definition of freedom to me is *living in your truth.*

In the movie *8 Mile* starring Eminem, he rapped about being everything but a child of God. Lo and behold, his opponent didn't have any ammunition to use against him in their rap battle. That's how I feel writing this book. I'm shedding light on the good, the bad, and the ugly, but it's a remarkable journey of my untold story.

The Real Mrs. Clause

Waking up on Christmas Day at my mother's house was always a blessing, but to be totally honest, all I could think about was going to my grandmother's house. Now, don't get it twisted, my mother always held it down and made sure we had everything we needed and a little bit of what we wanted. Being a single mother of three was never easy, but somehow she managed to always make it happen.

I can recall one Christmas when I received a ThunderCats toy set, a Knight Rider big wheel, a Hulk Hogan action figure with the wrestling ring included, and a mini soft basketball and rim set I could hang on my bedroom door. The rest were school supplies, clothes, and Nike shoes. Mom always made sure we had some fly gear if nothing else. Most of all, she made sure I was fully aware that she was the one who purchased my clothes and toys. Especially since I was the youngest, still running around believing in Santa Claus. I remember my mother overhearing me tell a friend that Santa brought me a big wheel. Man, was she hot! I can still hear her saying it in my head, *"Jae-Jae, ain't no such thing as no damn Santa Claus. I worked my ass off to pay for your Christmas!"*

I didn't understand then, being that I was around five or six years old, because all the kids I went to school with talked about Santa coming to town. I understand now, and I would never tell my own child(ren) that Santa Claus is real. My mother was right. *Why should he get the credit for something I worked my butt off to buy?* Nope, not going to happen. Some people say you should allow a child to be a child, and when the time is right, they'll eventually find out the truth. Even though Santa didn't make it to my mother's house, I bet you I knew whose house he *did* make it to.

My aunt Elvira would send my aunt Joyce or my aunt Angie to drive over to my mother's house later that evening to pick me up. Trust and believe, I would already be packed and waiting by the door. I could feel the energy of my sister piercing through the back of my neck, like, *I can't stand his spoiled tail.* That's right, I was spoiled, and I couldn't wait to get where I needed to be so I could be the center of attention. Upon arriving, my aunt would have the entire house lit up with beautiful Christmas lights. You could always spot the Christmas tree in the window. I have never in my life seen her with a fake Christmas tree. She was official! She never did anything half done or fake.

Of course, when I entered the house, I noticed the lit tree full of presents, candy canes, bows, and ornaments. At the bottom... let's just say it was fully loaded with gifts that my aunt said were from none other than the man of the hour…Santa Claus. I would always look at my aunt and wait for the go-ahead before I began opening presents, because nine times out of ten, she wanted to take a picture first. I would open present after present, after present. When I tell you, I felt like the luckiest kid on the planet…

My aunt Elvira loved her some Jae-Jae. I know now that she got her satisfaction from seeing a smile on my face. I didn't realize it back then, but now that I'm older, I honestly can't believe that God blessed me, out of all people, with such a beautiful soul to be around for life. Not only was she a beautiful soul, but she loved everyone, including her other nieces and nephews as well, but you had to be living under a rock if you didn't know I was her baby boy.

She could also cook, and her baking skills were amazing. I can't forget about her pineapple upside-down cake with a side of Breyers peach or vanilla bean ice cream. That combination was to die for. I've had several pineapple cakes since, but none have tasted, or even come close, to anything like my aunt Elvira's. Hands down, she could've sold that recipe to Martha Stewart. I can't wait until the day we're reunited. It'll be my time to watch both of my mothers open up present, after present, after present…the way they so rightfully deserve.

To know my aunt Elvira was to love her. Thank you so much, Auntie, for your unconditional patience, love, and understanding. Also, thank you for some of the most amazing Christmases a kid could ever imagine. You were, and have always been, in my heart...The Real Mrs. Clause.

My Aunt Joyce

My aunt Joyce called me Biddy Boy. For as long as I can remember, she's always stayed around the corner from my aunt Elvira. It was always a fun time at her house. Aunt Joyce used to have real slushy and ice cream machines in her kitchen and she always kept big snacks, cold milk, and plenty of boxes of Apple Jacks, Cap'n Crunch, and Fruity Pebbles on top of her refrigerator. I loved walking around the corner to visit. Most of the time, her husband, Donald Smith, aka "Duck," would take me out to Hickory to play ball with his family and friends. He was a killer on that blacktop. His game shaped and inspired mine in so many ways, and I'm forever grateful to have had his presence in my life.

My aunt Joyce, his wife, taught me how to drive a stick without physically teaching me. You can actually learn from observing. After years of watching her, one night I gathered up the nerve to take her keys to her Honda hatchback. It had to be around three in the morning. I remember not starting it up in the driveway. I just released the brake and it rolled down. Then, I put it in first gear, eased off the clutch while giving it a little gas, and before you knew it, I was flying down Portland Street at three in the morning doing about fifty miles an hour.

So yeah, Aunt Joyce, I got you too! Nobody was exempt when it came to Jae-Jae's adolescent ways. To be honest, even though it was wrong to steal her car, I could actually drive better than most adults at my age. So, your car was safe with me. I just took it for a light spin.

I got an amazing deal on my second car because it was a stick. When people would ask me how I learned to drive one, I'd always say, *"From watching my aunt. She was the best."*

Blue Velour & Bloodshed

It was the winter of 1996. I remember buying my first blue velour sweatsuit from a popular store in Military Circle Mall called *Up Against The Wall*. I was just passing by when I noticed the place was packed, so I walked in and was blown away by the newest fashion statement everybody was talking about. I copped two sets, then walked over to Foot Locker and grabbed a pair of the newly released blue and white Air Force Ones to match.

That winter felt different, though, because my brother was no longer here. He had just been sentenced to serve twenty-three years in the Virginia Department of Corrections. So, spending money and shopping became my personal therapy. I felt alone. My brother had always been my protector. I know for a fact I wouldn't have even thought about being in these streets or selling drugs if he were home.

Tee-Tee was a humble soul. All he wanted to do was work, buy clothes, drive cars, and talk to girls. His fashion sense was on another level. I gotta admit, he taught me everything I know. To me, he was one of the flyest dressers I've ever known, and it wasn't just the outfits. It was *how* he put them together. Every time I shopped, I'd ask myself, *Would bro wear this shirt with these pants?* I missed the hell out of my brother. To be honest, I didn't know how I was gonna make it through life without his guidance. I just knew I had to survive in these Uptown streets, no matter what.

A year later, I was living out in Virginia Beach with my homeboy's aunt, Kim. I was doing numbers and copping weight regularly from my new connect. After getting tired of cooking every other day, Kim was more than happy to teach me step-by-step how to cook and stretch cocaine. If I'm being real, that was the main reason I started dealing with her in the first place. I had just turned eighteen, and she was thirty. Kim never talked down to me or treated me like a youngin'…at least not how folks Uptown would joke about her and younger dudes. Except for one thing… every time we argued, she'd throw in, *"That's that young nucca sh*t."

I hated that.

I wasn't too young to be smashing or paying bills. Other than that, she was cool. Relationships take time and adjustments. I figured we'd work it out, but I'll never forget that day. I pulled into her driveway and saw her child's father standing beside his beat-up old Ford Explorer, talking to her. Kim's body language said it all. They weren't just catching up. She was grinning ear to ear and this was the same dude she swore she couldn't stand. Her exact words: *"I can't stand his black ass."*

Yeah, right.

I rolled down the window of my LS400 and asked him politely if he could move so I could park in my space. He looked me dead in the face and said, "F**k you!"

I laughed at the clown and kept pushing. I knew he was salty. He knew I had more money than him and I was smashing his baby mama.

I remember him saying, *"I got a son older than that nucca. I'll put his little ass over my lap and beat him."*

Of course I wanted to say something, but honestly? Time was money, and he wasn't worth either. What really got me, though, was that Kim never checked him. She never stood up for me. That's when I knew that my time in that relationship was ticking down, but I didn't expect the clock to run out that fast.

After a long day hustling Uptown, my pockets were right. I just wanted to shower, eat, and get a nice back rub before knocking out. That's exactly how the night went…until it didn't. I was deep in sleep and curled in the fetal position. Kim was stretched out across the bed and sleeping sideways. I didn't even realize what was happening until I opened my eyes and saw her baby daddy standing over her—and then,

BOOM! BOOM! BOOM!

He shot her three times.

Right in front of me.

I couldn't move. It was like my legs froze.

Then, he turned and pointed the gun at me. His eyes were wide like I was the real target all along, but God was with me. My praying grandmother must've been working overtime because he pulled the trigger twice…*click, click.*

The gun jammed.

I jumped out the bed and ran several houses down to call the police. I wasn't about to let her die on my watch. I remember seeing him speed by in his truck, hauling ass. I ran back and found Kim lying in a pool of her own blood, crying. Minutes later, the ambulance and police pulled up. I played it smart. When the detectives started asking questions, I turned into a little kid on them. Told them I didn't know what happened to my "auntie," said I was in my room playing video games when I heard the shots. One detective said there were no signs of forced entry, so whoever it was either had a key or was let in.

That hit different.

We had top-of-the-line locks and a working ADT alarm system. *Why would he shoot her?* They were just out front laughing and talking earlier. Then, it all started to click. The day before Kim got shot, we sat for hours counting up something light and loaded it into my safe. I truly believe it was a setup. A robbery gone wrong. Those three bullets he put in Kim were meant for me. I believe that with my whole heart.

As soon as the detectives left, so did I. Never went back.

There's no morality, no love, and no loyalty in the drug game. We live day by day and pray we see another. That night took a part of me, but that's not the end of my story...

Getting Back On My Feet

Thanksgivings were epic... I mean everyone in the family would show up at Grandma Odessa's house. Cars would overpack the driveway and the yard. Just pulling up, you knew who was already there. I had uncles and cousins from out of town who came through, especially ones I hadn't seen in years, like my uncle Rob and his wife Jennifer, Uncle Darry, my cousins, Astrine and Andrea, and their mother, my aunt Gina. They all lived in Northern Virginia. My cousins, AlJay and Jeffrey, came from New York, and Mark and David were from Maryland. Then, there was my cousin Keena and her sister Toya out of Elizabeth City, North Carolina. Somehow, out of all those family members, I always seemed to be the center of attention, mostly because of my love for Michael Jackson.

Once everybody's bellies were full, it was time to trip off Biddy Boi. My Uncle Dwight would call me into the den where he and a bunch of family members were sitting around watching the football game. He'd say, "Biddy Boi, give Unk a little bit of everything, since it's halftime." Mannn, when that music came on, I danced like I was trying to get the golden buzzer on America's Got Talent. I mean, for a kid, I could really jam. I remember looking up and seeing everybody laughing and cheering me on, and that's when I realized at a young age that I was special.

    I remember watching Michael Jordan and the Chicago Bulls play on TV. I was inspired. I really thought he could fly. My uncle Donald had two VCR tapes. One was called *Come Fly With Me* and the other was *Michael Jordan's Playground*. I must've watched them both over a hundred times. I was so fascinated and inspired by him. I actually became a decent hooper. Not many boys my age could match up with me on the blacktop. I was starting to see the greatness in me at an early age, but only if I could stay the course.

    The basketball courts Uptown felt like events in the summer. Everybody sported the latest fashion along with the newest Nike Air Jordans just to play ball in. The craziest part was, we could never get a good run in. Every five minutes, someone would stop the game to serve a dope fiend. The rest of us just stood there sweating. At first, I hated it. Then, I realized it was just part of Uptown culture. Luckily, I wasn't as easily influenced as my aunts and uncles thought I was. I had more opportunities than anybody I knew Uptown who sold drugs at a young age. My sister's boyfriend was the real plug, but all I wanted to do was play ball, drive cars, and talk to cute girls like my brother Tee-Tee. It just took money for all of that.

    Summer of 2001, I had just turned twenty-one and linked up with my cousin. Would you believe that just two weeks in, I ended up caught in a drug raid? I had never in my life sat in a trap, and for the life of me, I didn't know what I was thinking. I remember hearing a loud thump on the porch. Then someone said, "Norfolk Police." I just laid down on the floor and waited. Later that evening, I was booked and charged with multiple gun charges, possession with intent to distribute, and two manufacturing charges. I was punch drunk, but lucky for me, I was a first-time offender. Nobody, and I mean nobody, came to my aid or any of my court hearings except my mom. After that, I knew I was in this all by myself.

My bond was thirty-five thousand, and believe it or not, I sat in jail until I went to trial. My mother was the only person who sent me money every week for commissary. I survived on breakfast trays, ramen noodles, Dunkin Sticks, and oatmeal cakes. After serving one year and eight days, I was released on January 15th at midnight through a back door. There was no warm welcome waiting… just cold and windy rain hitting me in the face... but it felt amazing. I began my journey walking to my mother's house with nothing but the clothes on my back and a determined mind.

My mom was already waiting when I got there. She gave me the biggest hug and kiss ever, and my mother has never been an affectionate woman. That's how I knew she missed me. She had a hot dinner plate ready… fried chicken breasts, mac and cheese, mashed potatoes and gravy, and some buttery grand biscuits... the fluffy joints. Mannn, that food tasted like heaven. It didn't stand a chance. My mom sat and watched me eat like I hadn't eaten in years. I remember her laughing and saying, "Boy, you better keep your ass out of jail." Then, she passed me two hundred dollars and said that's all she had for the moment. I passed it back and told her I was good, even though I wasn't. She had already done more than enough, but somehow I knew that I was going to get back.

I was court-ordered to report to Potomac Job Corps in Washington, DC. I didn't want to go, but I knew if I didn't, I'd be back in jail. I never thought Job Corps would turn out the way it did. When I arrived, it was nothing like I imagined. At first glance, it looked like a prison. It was gated with only one entrance, but once you got inside, it looked like a college campus. The chicks were everywhere…to think I was sent there for punishment.

When I got off the bus, everybody stopped to see if they knew any of the new arrivals. Right away, within seconds, I heard a female ask, "Is that Jae-Jae." I looked up and it was my friend Tiffany from Uptown with a group of girls.

I replied, "Black... you already know!"

I got with Tiffany right after my orientation, and she hooked me up with her cute friend from Philly named Melody. To be honest, she was the baddest chick on campus, hands down. She was Cuban, Black, and Jamaican. I couldn't wait to get to know her. When I finally did, I found out she was the plug.

Potomac Was Lit

I was roommates with this cool twenty-year-old named Roger. He was from Israel. I thought that was an odd name for an Arab. I later found out he was adopted by a white couple after both of his parents died in a store robbery gone bad. He said he was seven years old when they named him. I used to joke him all the time about that saying, "Them white people named you that mess on purpose!" He would instantly get upset and tell me that, as soon as he turned twenty-one, he was changing it back to Amad-El Shyhid.

"Damn right," I would reply. "Them white folk crazy as hell naming you that."

Roger was book smart. He was attending Job Corps voluntarily, majoring in business administration. His parents had left him a chain of convenience stores in their will and testament. Altogether, it was a total of seven, with three in New York, three in Virginia, and the last one, their biggest store, located in Charlotte, NC. Roger was cool. He kept offering me a job to work at a couple of his locations whenever I left the Job Corps. He even talked about franchising me a few, but at that particular time in my life, to be honest, I had no clue what the hell Roger was talking about. I just knew I wasn't going to be working in nobody's Tinee Giant corner store.

Melody would always stop by the dorm to see me. All the guys would ask how I managed to pull her and I would always say she chose me, because she did. Tiffany said Melody wouldn't stop asking her about me, so she had to hook us up. I've always dated cute girls, so it wasn't nothing new to me. Mel knew that. She said I was different because her last boyfriend was clingy, but I could see why. Mel was definitely a keeper. I liked how she didn't allow her financial status to play a role in her personality or in our relationship. I was intrigued by her calm demeanor. She never complained or whined about anything. She was always positive, and she laughed at all my jokes... she was super silly. I could see why people loved being around her. Her fashion sense was through the roof. We were that power couple on the campus and for the next year, we had Potomac sold up with Mary Jane.

What goes up must come down.

Of course, people started hating and had the bozo campus security raid my room. They didn't find anything, but before they left, they told me they had their eyes on me.

Later, I found out who ratted me out. It was. This fake Jamaican named Kingston who owed me five hundred dollars, by the way. I was heated and wasn't thinking. As soon as I saw Kingston, I kicked his butt right in the cafeteria. Man, I flipped that place upside down. Potomac had a no-fighting policy, so I was kicked out the following day. Mel was upset at me, and I was too, because I had totally forgotten that I had been court-ordered to attend Potomac. Now, I was looking at my probation officer sending me back to jail, but this time, it wasn't going to be like the last time. I was determined to have my affairs in order.

      Every weekend, I would drive up to Washington, DC, and check into the Red Roof Inn to see Mel. Job Corps allowed students weekend passes to either leave the compound or go back home. Mel would check out for the weekend, and we would have the time of our lives. Money never played a factor because we had it. If I wasn't buying her something, she was buying me something. Mel was ending her last semester at Potomac in a few months and wanted me to move to Philadelphia with her. I was definitely down. She didn't even have to ask me twice. Two weeks later, we found out she was pregnant. I was elated about her being my child's mother, and to be honest, I was really looking forward to being a dad.

      The weather was beautiful when we landed in the City of Brotherly Love. We left the airport in a cab and began looking around the city for condominiums. Melody's bougie ass wanted a condo with two balconies. One, she wanted to be in the living room, and the other one had to be in our bedroom overlooking the city. Eventually, after looking at several, we found the condominium she loved. The rent was $2,250, no utilities included. Mel signed the lease, and our move-in date was the following week.

After we left the condo, we took another cab to her storage unit. I should've known something was up when she told the driver he could leave. We walked down a couple of units, and she stopped at Unit 121. I was expecting to see a bunch of furniture, but it was two vehicles parked with tarps covering them both. She asked me to help her take them off. When I did, I couldn't believe it. It was a black S500 Mercedes-Benz and a burgundy X5 BMW truck with burgundy rims. She reached in her pocketbook and tossed me the keys to the Benz, and we drove straight to the car wash and had them both washed and detailed. After we left the car wash, I followed Mel around West Philly as she gave me a grand tour of her city. I realized she was popular because everybody knew her. Every time, she would happily introduce me as her fiancé, and it felt good hearing that. I felt like the luckiest man alive.

    I was back in Norfolk handling business when I received a call from Tiffany asking if I'd heard from Melody. I told her I had just dropped her off at Potomac two days prior, and I hadn't called her because I figured she was in class finishing up the semester. Tiffany went on to say she was just informed that the Job Corps student van was in a tragic accident and that Melody was a passenger. When I asked if she was alright, she replied to me... there were no survivors.

    I put my head down and cried crocodile tears for the first time as an adult male. I couldn't believe I'd found my better half, and she was taken away from me just like that. That was another chapter in my book of life that affected me mentally and spiritually, but I learned to live, laugh, and love the way she would've wanted me to.

R.I.P. Melody Hernandez

Pg. 13 – I Can Always Bounce Back...

It's the summer of 2001, and I'm back Uptown. Somehow, I managed to sweet talk my probation officer into letting me work during the day and attend school at night. She agreed, but told me I had to check in with her once a week with a progress report from my teacher. She also wanted to see a weekly check stub. My intentions were never to do either, but I had to because Jones could've sent me back to jail. So of course, I went along with it. I went to my uncle Dwight and he hired me. Immediately, I began working at one of his warehouse locations.

Transitioning from selling drugs to working a job is like a drug addict going through withdrawal. I couldn't do anything with a three-hundred-dollar weekly check, even though I was offered as many overtime hours as I wanted. I couldn't take them because I had night classes to attend. Working at a warehouse, you meet people. I was on my lunch break, sitting in the parking lot, when I happened to link up with Tim. I'd been noticing him watching me for a while. He had seen me pull into the warehouse several times in my Q45t Infiniti. His curiosity got the best of him, and he approached me, asking why I was working in a pair of brand-new Jordans.

I laughed and said, "I didn't have any old ones."

We started chopping it up right there in the lot. I found out he was a dope boy on the come up from Chesapeake and was getting to the bag… just a lil' light. He told me his supplier had just gotten snatched up by the Feds, and he was searching for a new plug. I told him I knew someone I could call, but their prices were a little high.

I was testing him.

He replied like a typical dealer with his back against the wall. He said he wasn't tripping because he needed to keep his clientele. He told me he had twenty thousand cash and wanted to buy a brick of some decent cocaine. I gave him the dumbfounded look and said, "Twenty grand though?"

He said that was what he paid his last connect.

I looked him square in the face and said, "Your connect must've known El Chapo, giving you numbers that low."

He laughed and said that's probably because he copped a bird almost every two weeks from him. That made more sense. Then, I knew he had the money. I told Tim my guy might bite for thirty, but there was no way I'd even waste his time with a number that low. I acted like I was busy and told him to get back with me.

Rule number one, never let anyone know how much dough you hold. Biggie said it in the Ten Crack Commandments. **Rule number two**, never act like you're pressed for business. I was fly, flashy, and he knew my uncle owned the company, so of course I used that to my advantage. I made it look like I was doing more than I really was, and that I was going out of my way to help him. Before I reached my vehicle, he called me back.

"Okay," he said. "I can do the thirty grand. Just make sure everything is a hundred. I'm going half with somebody else."

I assured him it would be. He went to his car and sat for a few minutes. I knew he was counting money. He came back with thirty thousand cash. I told him I'd have his product when I returned to work in the morning. We shook hands, and I drove off overwhelmed with excitement because I knew I was about to bounce all the way back. Now, it was time to finesse my Uptown hustle. I made a few calls and ended up linking with one of my sister's ex-boyfriends, a Haitian named Justice. He always kept fish scale. I told him I was trying to get back on my feet and needed him to throw me a bone. I told him I wasn't coming empty handed, but all I had was fifteen grand to my name. Being the hustler I knew he was, he asked me exactly what I was trying to get. I told him a brick and a half, if he could do it. I was really just shooting for the brick. The half was for leverage.

He was quiet for a second, then replied, "I can probably do the brick, as long as you re-up and hit me on the back end."

"Bet," I replied.

We met up in the Wendy's parking lot. The exchange was made and the deal was sealed. I went back Uptown and found my runner, Albo. We stopped at Walmart for baking soda, then went straight to his spot. I watched him stretch one brick to a brick and a half like magic. I paid him one hundred dollars, a pack of Newport's, and an eight ball of powder for his services. Now, I was up a half a brick and fourteen thousand nine hundred dollars in a single day. If I ain't a hustler, what do you call that?

All facts.

The next morning, I got to work an hour early. I wanted to see who pulled into the lot. I didn't have time to get caught up in no sting. I sat in my rental and watched everyone arrive. Tim pulled up just like planned. His body language wasn't off and he didn't seem nervous at all. After five minutes, I pulled up beside him and we did the exchange. Believe it or not, he called me three days later wanting another brick. I couldn't believe it. For the next six months, this process went on and on. Before I knew it, I was back like I never left. Sometimes it's not what you know, it's who you know.

I had gotten all the way back, and I still showed up for work every day out of respect for my uncle. My probation officer, Jones, was short, thick, and sexy with a beautiful smile. One Saturday evening, I ran into her at the carwash. I paid for her wash and dinner with me at Captain George's. She promised to take me off papers, too. We stayed at the Holiday Inn…I slayed her all weekend for putting a G like me on probation in the first place.

I Got Me a Baddie

I was twenty-two and had everything going for me. I was even dating an older woman… again. Sonja reminded me of Tamron Hall with her short-cut hair and pretty smile. She was fifteen years my senior and had a daughter named Stephanie who was my age. Sonja was from New Jersey and had the sexiest accent ever. I was highly attracted to her, but for some reason, she questioned it daily. She would always ask me if I'd still love her fifteen years down the road when she was old and wrinkled. I'd be lying if I said I would, because the only thing I wanted old and wrinkled back then was some money. I always told her that looks fade, and it's all about the heart to me and to be honest, she didn't even look her age.

Sonja used to say things like, "Stephanie is the younger version of me, wasn't I a baddie, bae?"

I would never agree, even though Stephanie was definitely a baddie in my book. I used to think that was kind of weird, because now my woman had me picturing her as her daughter. I would say things to make her feel special like, "I love my women fine like aged wine."

Whenever Sonja and Stephanie would get into a heated argument, which was regularly, Stephanie would always ask me what made me want to be with her mother's old ass. It was always right in front of Sonja. I would always say, "Stephanie, keep me out of you and your mother's mess."

The day came when Sonja stormed into the house and, out of the blue, told me that I could no longer be in her house while she was at work. I was like, damn, I do pay bills around here, too. Then again, I wasn't on nobody's lease either. All I could think of was my mother in my ear years ago telling me to get my own house. Later, I found out she was upset that I gave Stephanie money to buy a few casual outfits for a job interview. She had a great job lined up, and I really didn't see anything wrong with it. I know you might think I was stupid or crazy for staying. You see, Sonja had twenty thousand stupid-crazy dollars of my hard-hustled money in her Bank of America account. At the time, I didn't want that much cash sitting around her house, and since she was my woman, I trusted her and asked if she could deposit it for me.

Sonja worked the night shift nursing and sometimes her hours were unpredictable. There were many nights I sat in my car until one or two in the morning waiting on her to come home. Most of the time, I would already be sleeping. She would pull up, tap the window, and go straight into the house to take a shower, wrap her hair, and go straight to sleep.

No, "Are you hungry?"
No, "How was your day?"
No, "You want some head?"
No, nothing.

I knew as soon as I got my money, I was going to ghost her ass. I was driving on a Saturday evening when I received a call from Stephanie. She was like, "I need to tell you something."

By the tone of her voice, I immediately pulled my car over. She went on to say that she was certain her mother was having an affair with another man who lived in Hampton. I asked her what made her tell me that because the two of them always seemed to be going at it. She said she would always ride or die with her mother, right or wrong, but when her demons started getting the best of her, it became toxic and unhealthy for them all. Somebody had to address it. Stephanie told me I was the first man she'd seen treat her mother right, and in return, her mother treated me the total opposite.

Not the official boy toy… again? I was done.

No more old bitches for me. It was my age or younger from this point on.

Now, I had to come up with a strategy, because Sonja wasn't going to drive to the bank and happily give me back my money, especially knowing I was leaving her. I knew Sonja too well for that. So, I had to come up with a plan I knew she would go for.

When you're a hustler, you always come up with a way to flip money. I told Sonja I needed her to take out a fifty-thousand-dollar loan from the bank so I could flip a foreclosed property we could potentially make up to a hundred grand return on. She asked why I wasn't using the money I had in the bank. I replied that I wanted to use that for bills and hard times. She was money-hungry, so I knew she would bite. She replied that she could probably get a loan for five grand, and I could add it to my twenty. I was like, anything beats a blank, but I needed it asap.

The day finally come, and we arrived at the bank. She had this dumb look on her face. I was like, "What's up?"

She admitted that she had withdrawn several grand out of the account, but planned to replace it with the loan she was about to take out. I acted like I didn't mind, but to be honest, I was heated. Seven grand was a lot of money to withdraw, especially when I was already helping with her bills. We walked out of the bank an hour later with twenty-five thousand dollars in cash. I wanted to speak my peace, but I was still playing it smart. We arrived home, and she supposedly got ready for work and said she would probably be getting off early to go see the property. I was like, "Cool, you're going to like it."

The minute she pulled out of the driveway, I started packing all my things as fast as I could. Stephanie walked in laughing and started helping me load everything into my car. I thanked her for everything and told her if she ever needed anything, to hit me up. I received a message from Sonja, screaming and calling me everything but a good man. I never replied to her again. I had my money and my own apartment now.

One year later, I received a call from Stephanie. She was living in a shelter in Portsmouth and needed a few dollars to get back and forth to her job. I agreed and told her to catch a cab to my spot. When she arrived, my heart almost beat through my chest because she looked identical to her mother. I answered the door, and she instantly gave me a big hug and a kiss.

I guess I got my young baddie after all.

Mi Castillo
After a long night Uptown hustling on the block, I arrived at my apartment around three in the morning, tired and hungry. I got to the door, and for some reason, my key wasn't working.

"The hell?" I recall saying.

I stepped back to check the address...because I was tired and could've been tripping...but I suddenly realized I wasn't. I called my girl's phone and it went straight to voicemail. I even walked around the corner to see if her car was parked in her space... and it was. All I could do was reflect on our last conversation about me coming home late every morning. I began knocking harder...this time more aggressively like the police.

Still no answer.

I knew for a fact that if she was in the apartment, she would have heard me. I got back in my car, drove off, and headed to Norfolk. Just before I got off the exit, I received a text message that read:

> **Your clothes will be on the deck in the morning, and I changed my locks, by the way.**

This bitch! After I had just gone to Meyers & Tabakin with my mother and furnished an entire house and her poe ass pulls this stunt. I could always seek refuge at my mother's house. My cousins and I hung out there often. We called it the Bat Cave. I guess it was my mother's way of assuring me that, regardless of what happens in life, I could always come back home.

I entered and went straight upstairs. I rolled a blunt and fell asleep. I woke up overhearing my mother talking to her neighbor, Miss Bae.

"Gurl, I'm tired as hell. They done worked a sister like a damn slave today. I see Jae-Jae's ass still here..."

She had noticed my car hadn't moved. I hadn't realized it, but I had slept through the entire morning and evening.

My mother called my name, walking in.

I replied, "Yes!" Only because she hated it when anybody answered her with a "Huh."

"You okay?"

"Yes," I replied again.

She opened the door and said, "That girl put you out again, didn't she?"

All I could do was laugh. I could never trick my mom. She was upset with me, and I could tell. The day we went furniture shopping, she kept saying, *"You can afford your own house. Why don't you just do that, Jae-Jae? Stop being Captain Save-a-Hoe all the time. This is my third time helping you furnish another girl's house."*

She was right. I was a walking sugar daddy furniture lick, but when you're getting money, you tend to overlook things that others don't. I knew she was a Rent-A-Center chic. I just liked to be comfortable wherever I was. My mother went on to say that one of my first cousins was a traveling nurse and had been with the same client for over fifteen years. She said the client's daughter was deploying overseas to Germany, and all she knew was that the woman was going through a divorce and had a nice house out in Virginia Beach. It had been on the market for over a year, and she wanted to sell it to my cousin for a really good price for taking care of her mother, but my cousin had already purchased a new home earlier that year. My mom didn't know the specifics, but she said she'd talk to my cousin and see if she could hook me up.

I was like, "Cool, Mom. Just let me know."

Two weeks later, my cousin popped up at my mother's house unexpectedly. She said, "Yes, Jae-Jae! You would like the house. It's nice."

That's when she passed me her client's daughter's number and told me to give her a call. At first, I was hesitant. A nucca didn't even have a hundred on his credit score…not to mention a regular nine-to-five. All I had at the time was money.

Who in their right mind was going to sell a home to a young, Black twenty-five-year-old with those credentials?

A week passed, and I bumped into my cousin at the local Feather & Fin. She asked me if I had made the call. I told her I hadn't and explained how I felt about my lack of credentials. She told me to try anyway. She said that the last time they spoke, Sabrina was down and out and needed money. She said it couldn't hurt and to let her know I was referred by her. The following Friday, I called. Sabrina answered on the first ring. I told her my name and that I was a student at Norfolk State University, and I was looking for a house for me and my family. I told her I'd viewed several properties and wanted to know if I could get a tour of hers. She was ecstatic and asked if Saturday morning was good for me. I said that was a great time, and we hung up. We both were looking forward to the following day.

Sabrina told me she'd be in a red Jaguar and would be parked at the Krispy Kreme on Virginia Beach Blvd. I pulled up five minutes late because I had a wake-and-bake and didn't want to smell like a Christmas tree. I arrived and noticed a woman sitting in a red car, but two things had me questioning.

One, what kind of car was she in? It didn't look like the Jaguars I'd been seeing lately…if it even was one.

Two… she was a white woman. She sure didn't sound white, and her name was Sabrina. So, I sat back in my car and waited patiently.

She stepped out of her car to head into Krispy Kreme, wearing a tight red dress and a pair of six-inch stilettos. When I tell you this Caucasian woman shook the concrete when she walked... just know I couldn't keep my eyes off her.

When she came out, our eyes locked. She started walking toward my car.

This weed got me tripping, I thought.

I rolled my window down, and she said, "Jae-Jae?"

I replied, "Yes."

She laughed and said, "I'm Sabrina."

I looked confused. She laughed again and said, "You thought I was a Black woman on the phone. I get that a lot."

I was thinking more like... *that ain't the only thing I noticed that's Black about you, baby,* but I kept that to myself. Sabrina was a cutie too, with her short Halle Berry-style haircut. I began lusting so hard that I almost forgot the reason I was even there. Then, she asked me to follow her.

We pulled out of the parking lot and drove about a quarter mile north before making the first left into a newly developed community. These houses were tucked away. You had to know about them because you wouldn't just stumble across this neighborhood. From the looks of it, the homes ranged anywhere from $450,000 to over a million dollars. I followed Sabrina down a few streets until we reached Sunny Trail Lane. It was a mixed community, more Black families than white, from what I could tell, and it was clean. I mean spotless. You couldn't find a piece of paper on the ground if you tried.

As we drove through, everyone waved. I saw white folks watering their grass and black folks washing their cars. It was a beautiful neighborhood. Then, Sabrina made a right into the driveway of a gorgeous brick home with a two-car garage. The first thing that caught my eye was the golden chandelier hanging through the upstairs window. I parked my Lexus beside her Jaguar, and we both stepped out. This time, we were standing face-to-face. I couldn't believe how short and thick she was in those heels. I had to get my mind right and remind myself I was here to see the house, not her.

I decided to cut to the chase and asked, "How much are you asking for the house?"

"Three seventy-five," she said. "It was listed for four-fifty, but I'm just ready to move on and leave the memories behind."

That had me thinking something tragic had happened here, but she explained that while she was deployed overseas working in the military, she found out through a mutual friend that her husband had been living a double life. Another woman had been living in the house the entire time she was away.

She said he thought she'd be overseas for three more months, but she said, "I 0-7'd off the ship and popped up on them and found them in bed watching Netflix."

She was devastated.

I wanted to hug her... to say something comforting… but all I could manage was, "I'm sorry to hear that."

She said she was good now and that she'd gotten the house and a few cars in the divorce.

I told Sabrina I thought it was a rent-to-own situation and apologized for wasting her time.

She shook her head. "I wish it could be. I'd do it, but I'm moving out of the country." Then, she added, "But I've got your number. If that becomes an option and you're still interested, I'll call you."

Two weeks later, my cousin Monica stopped by my mom's house. She was on the hunt for someone selling food stamps. I happened to be pulling up as she was leaving. She asked what happened with the house.

I said, "She wanted three seventy-five."

"You tell her I referred you?" Monica asked.

I paused. "I didn't, Cuzz."

She told me, "Call her back and let her know the count."

That night, I called Sabrina. She answered on the second ring. "Hello, Jae-Jae!"

I greeted her and explained that Monica Davis had referred me.

"Monica? Oh my GOD!" she said. "She's like my sister."

She went on and on about how Monica had been her mother's caretaker for over fifteen years and how her mom wouldn't let anyone else take care of her. "Your cousin is sweet and honest," she said. "People like her are rare in nursing nowadays."

Then, out of nowhere, she asked, "How much can you afford a month?"

I had no clue what to say. "Whatever you're asking," I replied.

She laughed. "I know you're in college and have a daughter. How about nine a month?"

"Nine thousand is a little steep," I said, halfway joking.

She burst out laughing. "No! Nine hundred a month. I needed that laugh."

I told her I could manage that.

She said, "Meet me at the house tomorrow. We'll go over the paperwork."

I hung up in disbelief. I'd spent $900 on drinks in the club…and I didn't even drink. This couldn't be real. I just knew she was going to ask for my bank info and a credit report. If so, I'd be hit like good dope on a Sunday. I was up early. I remembered Monica saying Sabrina had been struggling lately and behind on daycare and storage bills. I went into my safe and pulled out $10,000 in cash for the deposit, just in case she asked for a credit check. I figured money might speak louder. I stopped by my mom's to see if she needed anything. She didn't. I told her I was about to put a down payment on a house. She didn't believe me until I showed her the money.

"Jae-Jae, you can't give that woman that damn money like that," she said.

She hopped in the car, and we drove to the post office, where I bought ten $1,000 cashier's checks. What was once stuffed in a duffel bag, now sat neatly in an envelope. "That looks more professional," my mom said.

I pulled up to the house around ten. Sabrina was already there. Music was playing. The fireplace was lit. Scented candles burned, and my favorite Pillsbury cookies were hot and ready. It felt like she was setting the tone for something more, but I had to stay focused. She hugged me this time. I nearly melted. She pulled out a stack of paperwork…her copies and mine. Then, she said we'd do a maintenance tour to make sure everything was in working order. It was. The house was only three years old.

After the tour, I signed everything.

"Congratulations, Jae-Jae," she said, handing me the keys.

In return, I gave her the envelope. She opened it, and instantly, tears welled up in her eyes.

I hugged her for real this time, and with good intentions because I was happy as hell too. Sabrina had really just blessed me with a four-bedroom, three-and-a-half-bathroom, upstairs-downstairs, two-car garage home. Man, I knew my life was about to do a one-eighty.

She proceeded to go over all the Western Union information with me and instructed me on how to wire the rent payments. She shook my hand and congratulated me before walking out. I stood in the doorway in awe, waving goodbye, saying to myself, *This can't be real.* She's going to come back and ask me for some kind of proof of income, credit score, bank information…better yet, an ID, but she didn't. I watched her drive all the way down Sunny Trail Lane until she disappeared. I felt like Macaulay Culkin in *Home Alone*. I ran up and down the stairs yelling at the top of my lungs, "I got my own house!"

Mannnn, it felt amazing.

That entire morning, I stayed there waiting for her to return. I even checked my phone several times, until I came to the realization, it was really all mine. After analyzing the entire situation, I realized Sabrina didn't do any of that for *me*. All of that was off the strength of my cousin Monica for being such a good person and taking care of Sabrina's mother. It didn't matter who I was or how much I could afford. If Monica sent me, I was golden in her eyes. She knew if anybody had her back, it would be Monica. I felt honored that Cousin Monica trusted me enough to put her name behind me. That was a monumental trump card she pulled out of the deck. It just goes to show, you can never put a value on being a good person. You never know how your good deeds can affect the people around you in ways unimaginable.

I walked outside to the driveway and got in my Lexus. I was pulling into my new garage for the first time… breaking it in. I noticed the other vehicle space was empty and needed to be occupied, so why not splurge on me?

I had it!

It was time to spoil me for a change. I'd been taking care of everyone in my circle and had been coming up on the short end every time. A week prior to getting my house,

Derrick, my car salesman over at Fly Rides, called to tell me he had the Q45t Infiniti model I'd inquired about. At that time, I told him I didn't even have a roof over my head, so I'd have to get back with him. Now that I had an official garage to park it in, there was no way I wasn't going to buy it.

I called my boy and told him I was coming through to pick him up, and we drove over to Derrick's car lot early Saturday morning around ten. There she was.

I had finally met my baby girl.

I named her *Unique*.

She was a big-bodied, champagne-colored beauty with dark tints. Derrick said he only had it a couple of weeks and was asking $20,000 cash or $30,000 if I financed it.

I looked at him like he was a retard. This wasn't my first purchase. Derrick was acting up. I knew for a fact he probably got it at the auction for around ten to fifteen grand. I offered him seventeen grand, take it or leave it.

Let's just say, I drove my Q45t *Unique* back home and parked her in my garage beside my LS430 *Niomi*. Now, I was living big dawg status for real. I just had to stay humble and lay low, because nuccas be hating, and I knew them streets would definitely be watching.

Jacked by a Jack Boy...

Yeah... I bet you've probably heard a hustler or two say they've never been robbed before, right? Well, that could only mean one thing…they weren't getting enough money! In the drug game, it's never an unscathed road to the top. There's always another side to it.

We were all taught the pros and cons, or the causes and effects, in school. Your thoughts, ways, and actions all have causes and effects. Those thoughts, ways, and actions would always return to their original source, YOU, times ten…good or bad. It's the law of the universe... and guess what? Nobody is exempt. That's why you see a lot of dope boys doing good deeds in their communities. They know they're killing their people, so they're just trying to soften the blow when their time comes knocking.

I was told by an old head back in the day, *"Jae-Jae, for every one dope boy that's getting money, it's a thousand jack boys out to get him."*

That statistic alone was alarming. It let me know I was a walking lick... or a dead man in just a matter of time because you never know how rational, or irrational, the jack boy is thinking in that situation, especially if he doesn't get what he wants. I could've never imagined that day would come true for me, but when it did, it changed me forever…

My morning started regularly…me driving through the city in my Q45t, listening to Jim Jones' *P.O.M.E.*, picking up money, dropping off packs, smoking blunts, and eating fast food. I needed a fresh pair of wheat Timberlands and a Polo for an upcoming event at the Funny Bone, so I decided to make a quick pit stop at the mall. I'd already collected a substantial amount of money, so before I exited my vehicle, I grabbed a stack of all hundreds and put the rest in the trunk.

When I entered Foot Locker, it was packed like they had a new Jordan release or something. I realized it was a back-to-school sale when I saw all the kids running around. I already knew what I wanted, so after getting my Timbs, I stood in line. In front of me was this sexy, slim-thick Puerto Rican with a pretty little Spanish daughter. I overheard her telling another female that her daughter's father was a deadbeat, and she was doing everything by herself. I noticed she had on a Wendy's uniform. Then, I looked at what she had on the counter. It was kid stuff…maybe around two hundred dollars tops. I asked her if it was okay if I paid for her daughter's clothes and shoes. She was like, "Sure... and thank you."

    I stepped in front of her and told the clerk I was covering everything. The lady at the register said, "That's so sweet of you," and I told her it was somethin' light. I pulled out a wad of money and counted out four hundred dollars. The second I put the money back in my pocket, I made eye contact with a man sitting on a bench across from me. I'm very observant, and off the rip, I noticed he didn't have any bags or even a single shoe in his hands. My gut told me he was down on me. I had to scrap my plan to get her number. The feeling I was getting told me to hurry up and get the hell out of Foot Locker. I started scoping out exit options, and that's when I noticed another dude standing by the door, looking just as suspicious. I decided to walk out with the crowd and head straight to my car.

    I kept looking back. I didn't see him behind me. My phone rang, and as soon as I answered it, *out of nowhere*, another man walked up, put his left arm across my shoulder, and jammed a pistol in my ribs with his right hand like he was trying to crack them.

    I knew he was serious. This wasn't his first rodeo.

    I couldn't believe he was actually robbing me... *in the mall.*

    He gritted his teeth and said, "If you utter one word, I'm going to kill you in this f***in' mall. Now, where's the money?"

    I complied and pointed to my pocket. I wasn't gonna say nothing! He damn near ripped my jeans off getting to it. He took my Timberlands and pushed me in the opposite direction before he dipped out. I stood in the middle of the mall in total shock. I couldn't believe the boldness. Six hundred dollars and a pissy pair of Timberlands… that's all he got.

I was just glad I had it to give, and that I walked away with my life. I left Military Circle Mall for the last time. I promised myself I'd never shop there again. I drove to Lynnhaven Mall in Virginia Beach and re-bought my outfit and Timbs, but it wasn't the same. Shopping felt… different.

It's not just the innocence in children that can be taken away. It can be *anything* that affects a person negatively for the first time. That jack boy took away my innocence that morning. Shopping was no longer fun for me. I felt uncomfortable being around too many people. Instead of enjoying myself, I was watching my surroundings and everybody around me.

I told my cousin everything, *in grave detail.*

The first thing he said was, "You need a pistol." He went on to say, "You getting too much money to be drivin' around the city all nilly-dilly like you ain't got a target on your back!"

I had to admit, I was nervous about having a gun, but more anxious than anything. Later that day, I met back up with him. He handed me my first strap. It was an all-chrome, top-of-the-line Smith & Wesson 9mm Ruger with two clips and a pearl handle. For the life of me, I just couldn't get that jack boy's face out of my head. I couldn't stop thinking about how many bullets I wanted to put in him if I ever saw him again. Until then, nobody better give me a reason to *think* they were out to get me because, I promise you, in my mind state, I wasn't the same Jae-Jae anymore.

That day created a gun-toting, heartless, rebellious man... ready for *whatever.*

Badd Gun Energy!!

It was like ever since I purchased my gun, problems seemed to follow me. I can remember countless situations I was involved in just because I had a gun. I recall one incident where my cousins and I had just left the club and decided to stop by the Waffle House and grab a bite to eat. As soon as we entered, I noticed how congested it was. My cousins knew how much I hated crowded restaurants. Normally, if I couldn't get a seat facing the front entrance, I'd rather wait until the next available one. That was law for me.

My two cousins were like, "The hell with all that!" They kept stressing how hungry they were and weren't worried about anything happening. One of them said, "Just tell me what you want to eat, and I'll bring it out to the car."

Of course, I told him a steak and cheese omelet with an orange juice. I decided to roll up a blunt while I waited. The radio was lit that night, so I was locked in. I was listening to all the up-and-coming events happening in the Hampton Roads area that weekend. I lit the blunt and puffed it twice before I looked up and saw what looked like a brawl going down inside the restaurant.

Instantly, I reached under the seat of my rental car to grab my gun. I tried to exit quickly, but my seatbelt snagged me back. I believe that second saved me from being another Black man killed by the police, because, by the time I unbuckled and opened my door, several armed officers ran directly past my car and headed into the Waffle House. My heart almost fell out of my chest. Immediately, I started the car and drove as close as I could to the door.

To my surprise, both my cousins came running out. Once they got in, I asked, "What the hell y'all do?"

My younger cousin said he punched some dude in the face, and they got to rumbling over a spot in line. I shook my head. "That's why I knew not to go in there with you, especially when you been drinking." Cuzzo could be a dickhead when he's intoxicated.

I exited onto the interstate, driving the speed limit. I noticed the Virginia Beach blue and whites were everywhere. About a quarter mile up, I heard what sounded like gunshots. I looked over to my left, and that's when I saw it. Flames were firing from what looked like a gun. Somebody was actually shooting at us. I lost control of the vehicle for a minute and tried to get out of their path. When I regained control, I began shooting back…unloading both clips. That's when I saw their car start swerving toward the guardrail before hitting it head-on. My adrenaline kicked in, and I was about to stop and back up to finish them off, but my cousin urged me to keep driving.

By the time we got back Uptown, the sun was already rising. I told my peoples to return the rental back to the airport, and I went home. Later that afternoon, I saw on the news the footage of a suspected vehicle wanted in connection with a shooting of two individuals. The reporter said the injuries weren't life-threatening. I let out a breath of relief. I'd finally busted my gun cherry, and I couldn't even say it felt good at all. I wiped the gun clean, walked a couple blocks over, and threw it down a storm drain.

Immediately, I went and bought another gun. I didn't feel safe walking around without one. My cousin came over later and apologized for being stupid. He knew damn well we all could've gone down for that foolishness, but when you're living the street life, you know all the chaos come with it.

Would you believe that same day, me and the same cousin went to a local cookout?

Cuzzo started shooting dice, having the time of his life, and winning everybody's money. I could tell the tension around the game was building. He had the bank and was talking real slick and greasy like an Uptown nucca do. I couldn't tell him to grab his money and leave, because it's rules to the game. I play too, so I know. I quietly exited myself, something I didn't want to do, but I moved quickly and went out to the car, and gathered both our pistols. I came back into chaos. Just that fast, like I was saying, it's rules to the dice game, and Cuzzo had just cee-lo'ed, meaning he rolled a 4-5-6. That meant he could leave with everybody's money, fair and square. I was quiet the entire time, observing everybody's body language. When I realized they weren't going to let us leave, I pulled out both guns and dared anybody to act like they wanted it.

I overheard an older man say to the crowd, "Please let that young nucca with that gun go!!" He looked in my eyes and knew I wasn't playing no games.

Cuzz collected his winnings off the floor, and together, we exited from the back of the house, got in our vehicle, and drove off. I told Cuzz I was done going anywhere else with him. It had to be at least twenty people I drew down on. That's twenty people I had to watch out for wherever I went. Even though we were in the right, I knew it was wrong to pull guns on people, but I had to make sure we got out safe. So, as far as that situation goes... I don't regret it.

I did realize that ever since I started toting guns, I had been attracting more negative attention. I know now that **nothing good** can happen when it's **bad gun energy** you're projecting...but that's not the end of my story.

"The Streets Is Watching…"

Yeah, that's what Jay-Z said, and there's so much truth in that song. When you're in the streets, it's not just the cops watching you. The dope fiends, the jack boys, and sometimes even your own family have their eyes on your pockets. The hustling lifestyle, when I reflect back on it, was as sinister and chaotic as anything I've ever experienced.

I remember an older hustler I grew up knowing named Skeeno. He once told me, "For every one drug dealer getting money, there's a thousand jack boys waiting to take it."

Those were some astronomical numbers, and now I realize just how factual that statement really was. *Why would a jack boy risk selling drugs when he can rob you in sixty seconds or less for everything you hustled for all day?*

I've never met a jack boy, and I've grown up with plenty who had more hustle, ambition, or money than me. They might have looked the part with their designer clothes, nice cars, and expensive jewelry, but that was usually temporary. Eventually, they would run out of money and start selling the same jewelry, the car, or even their clothes. I witnessed it more than enough times. That happened because of their lack of discipline, hustle, and ambition. Once they went broke, they'd hit another lick, and it became a cycle. Eventually, their luck would run out. Karma would catch up with them. They would either get killed or end up in prison. Sadly, the outcome for both jack boys and drug dealers were often the same.

Jack boys want everything fast and easy, just like drug dealers, but the difference between them and a true hustler is this. You can rob a hustler for everything on him and everything in his pockets, and he will still bounce back.

That's because it's not what's on him. It's what's in him. That go-getter mentality is a rare breed. In the song *Pound Cake*, Jay-Z was told, "It's not many of us." He replied, "Less is more, nucca. It's plenty of us left."

That means the true hustlers are still out here and thriving. They just switched the game. Now, they're investing in businesses, stocks, and real estate. They're still cornering the market, still making money, but now, they're creating generational wealth and financial freedom.

I remember when Skeeno finally sold me my first eight-ball of crack. I looked at him like he was Mitch. He always had on a butter leather jacket and some fresh-out-the-box Air Force Ones. He drove several cars, but I couldn't take my eyes off that gold Acura Legend. When I was younger, I used to ask him for a dollar every time I saw him. Without hesitation, he would dig in his pocket and hand it to me. I always noticed his big bankroll, but I still only asked for one dollar. He once told me he liked that about me. Skeeno saw something in me back then that I hadn't yet seen in myself, but it was only a matter of time.

You could tell how long his drug run was because I'd known him since I was a kid, and now I was a teenager buying from him. I remember paying sixty dollars for that first eight-ball. At that time, all the boys my age Uptown were already selling quarters and ounces. I had been spoiled my whole life and didn't really have to hustle, but back then, it seemed like the cool thing to do. Growing up in the early nineties, drug dealers weren't looked at as bad people. They had this image like they were hood celebrities. Only our grandmothers saw them as a cancer to the community. To us, it was as if they had made it out the hood without ever leaving it.

My cousin Montreal was in my room playing Madden, rolling a Philly blunt, when I came busting in showing off my eight-ball like it was a brand-new Rolex. He laughed and said, "It's a hundred of y'all lil' nuccas scoring from Skeeno, posted up in the same neighborhood, standing on the same block, and selling the same crack. It might take you a week to sell that lil ass eight-ball."

He was right. Everybody Uptown was buying from Skeeno. He told me the only way I was going to move my pack was if my rocks were bigger than everyone else's. That meant my usual profit of two-fifty would drop to one-fifty. He grabbed a plate and started cutting up some of the biggest dime rocks I'd ever seen.

He said, "It's all about your turnover rate. If you do this three times a day, I guarantee you'll make more money than the rest of your crew. You just have to keep your business to yourself."

Would you believe he was right?

Crackheads were walking past crowds of dealers to get to me. My friends couldn't figure it out, but I kept my mouth shut. Just like Montreal predicted, I started spinning circles around them. Soon, instead of buying from Skeeno, they were buying their product from me. I started to get creative. I was still buying my beige-colored crack from Skeeno, but I added food coloring to make it look like something totally different. My *personal* crack was still selling out. Not because of the color, but because of the size. I ended up getting most of the money my peers would normally give to Skeeno because they thought what I had was better. It was really his crack the whole time…just a different color.

Since I was bringing Skeeno so much money, he started wholesaling me weight at a cheaper rate. I learned how to corner the market at a young age. One thing about Uptowners, we always say, *"If you can trick 'em, you can beat 'em."*

I adopted that phrase and used it to my advantage. Not to cheat, but to always stay ahead because no matter how high you rise, the streets were always watching.

Working Man

I had been living in my home for about six months, and everything was going well. I had finally gotten adjusted to the single life and living by myself. My landlord, Sabrina, was ecstatic about getting her rent payments months in advance. I had even begun a little interior decorating. Even though I wasn't home much, I still needed it to have a *home-like* feeling. I was driving past The Dump, a local furniture store, one afternoon when I decided to make a U-turn.

Upon entering, I noticed people looking at TVs, rugs, and sectionals. I didn't have a clue what I was looking for. I wished my mother was with me, but I wanted to show her I could do this house thing on my own. So, I purchased the first leather sectional I saw. It was a butter-soft raspberry color, and the tag read $3,500. I purchased it. The clerk notified me of the delivery date and time, and it was on.

To this day, I have no clue why, but I stopped at Spencer's in the mall. Yo, I balled out. I mean, I purchased everything from Scarface coffee tables, along with orange and lime green lava lamps, New Orleans Saints shower curtains, floor mats, keychains, and dishware. As soon as I left Spencer's, I stopped at Best Buy and purchased a PlayStation, an Xbox 360, and a Sony movie projector. My luxury home resembled nothing more than a man cave, but it was mine, and that was all that mattered to me.

I started back working for my uncle Dwight at Genesis Staffing from eight in the morning to five in the evening. The job atmosphere was relaxed. Everyone was cool. Every morning, we had fresh coffee and donuts from Krispy Kreme, or turkey bacon, egg, and cheese biscuits from Hardee's, available in our office kitchen. I was starting to become a fat boy working there. My uncle wasn't my uncle at work, so I didn't ask him certain questions or expect him to do certain things. Even though I still got away with everything imaginable, I loved the fact that he gave me some leverage and the opportunity to learn and experience business administration at the forefront.

I was the person who handled the hiring process. I was trained by Mrs. Debbie, the Chief Financial Officer for our company. She had been a part of the company since my uncle launched his business. Once a person submitted their job application, I would make a copy of their identification and highlight their job description. All forklift drivers went in this file, and all material handlers went in the other file. Then, I logged it into the computer.

Apples and oranges, right?

Hiring would only begin whenever the warehouse distribution centers like H.U.D., Dollar Tree, D.D. Jones, or Target would call our office for workers. Then, I was their man.

Ring, ring...

"Hello, this is Jae. We are having a wonderful day here at Genesis. How may I help you or redirect your call?"

I said this in my best professional voice. People would call all day asking if I could hire them, and I would tell them, be on standby if they had already submitted an application, because something should be available soon. The contracts we held with various companies at Genesis Staffing were all seasonal, and all of our employees knew they were only part-time positions.

As soon as I received the go-ahead from my supervisor, Gary, to begin hiring, I started calling all the chics like, "You still want a job, Tasha, Kim, or Ebony?"

Of course, they would all say yes. I would then say something like, "You know I went out of my way to get you this job. Your application was way in the back, so make sure you show up on time tomorrow at eight."

They used to be so excited, and of course, I would somehow sweet-talk my way into getting to know them outside of work. When people saw me in the streets, instead of asking for work such as drugs, they were actually asking me for a job. I felt like I was making a difference in my community. I hired everybody I knew from my neighborhood. I hired so many women that one day, my uncle walked into the office and said, "Jae-Jae, is it a possibility that you can start hiring some more men? Like, what are we doing here? I have a warehouse full of women who can't lift a kitchen table."

I was like, "Damn, Unk, my bad."

I snapped. I had to tighten up before Unk fired me... again.

I loved my job at Genesis. It was laid-back, even though Gary and Mrs. Debbie were nosy as hell. They knew from the way I carried myself that I had a second stream of revenue coming in. I never complained about anything. I did my assigned job every day and went home. Anything else outside of work was my business. Then again, I blame myself for not picking up my checks on Fridays like everyone else.

I had Fridays off, and it was more convenient for me to pick it up on Monday when I returned to work. I recall Mrs. Debbie asking, "What regular person does that?"

Like I said, I was there for the experience and the opportunity, not the salary. At that time, I could make in a day hustling, what I made in a week at Genesis Staffing. It wasn't about the money. I was actually learning a business skill that I knew would benefit me in the long run, but Mrs. Debbie was right on point because I've never been regular.

Back at home, I loved the fact that I could say I had a professional job. My neighborhood was a working-class community. Like clockwork, every morning, you knew when each person would be pulling out of their driveway. If I noticed, I knew they did too. So, even when I wasn't working, I developed a schedule for myself to leave every morning. If not, I would just park one of my vehicles in my garage.

I couldn't complain. Life was good whenever I was out at the beach, but when I crossed over into another city, it was always a tense situation. I was living two different lives, and man, it was starting to affect me. I wanted to leave the streets behind and continue working, but the money I was making couldn't pay half my rent or provide me with the lifestyle I was used to living.

When It Rains, it Pours...

I figured I would start putting money aside to start my own small business. A barbershop would be nice, but I quickly deaded that thought. I knew as long as I was active in the streets, I couldn't open up any legit businesses. I would've literally been a sitting duck for either the narcotics or the jack boys. I was tired of having to tote a pistol everywhere. I was taking a risk just doing that alone, especially being a convicted felon. The street life was literally tearing me apart... physically and mentally. There's no amount of money on this planet that could take the place of peace of mind, safety, and comfort. Three things I prayed for daily.

Universal law states that for every action, there is a reaction. For every cause, there is an effect. For every victory, there is always a sacrifice. I realized I sacrificed my peace of mind, safety, and comfort when I dedicated my time and energy to the streets. By doing that, I received everything I desired at the snap of a finger. My ultimate goal then was to find a smooth exit plan out of the game. I had a beautiful home, but never experienced a relaxing drive on my way to it. I always had to play with my mirrors just to make sure I wasn't being followed. The same went for my cars. As much as I loved them, I barely had time or the opportunity to drive them. Instead, I spent thousands of dollars on rental cars. I had several different names and identities. I just wanted to be regular again. I was to the point where I was willing to lose it all for a peace of mind.

DMX said, *"I sold my soul to the devil, and the price was cheap."*

Very cheap, because being happy is priceless. I had money, and I was more miserable now than I was when I was broke. I learned a valuable lesson. That was, I could never find true happiness in material things. I began to get down on my knees and pray daily, asking GOD for forgiveness. I started going back to work Monday through Thursday. I stopped selling drugs and carrying my gun. I had to figure a way out of the game because I was starting to feel like the devil wasn't finished with me just yet.

I was Uptown one Saturday night, enjoying myself at Gloria Maye's, a local bootlegger house in my hood. I'd been smoking weed and tripping off the drunk old heads who were telling me stories from back in the day. The night wasn't getting any younger, so I decided to call it. I had to be at work in the morning, and I still had a twenty-minute drive home.

I exited the house and began walking towards my car. The entire time, my gut feeling told me something wasn't right. I was about 10 feet from my vehicle when someone came out of nowhere and hit me in the back of my head with a brick. I wasn't sure, but it felt like it.

Instantly, I reached for my gun and remembered that I wasn't carrying it anymore. The jack boy told me to give him my money and jewelry, or he was going to shoot me. I quickly gave him what he wanted so he could leave. After he got what he wanted, he hit me again on top of my head with the gun and almost knocked me unconscious.

I was livid. All I remembered was lying on that cold ground, with my head bleeding profusely. Even though he was masked up, I recognized his walk immediately. I wasn't going to rest until I wreaked havoc on his azz. I wasn't getting any rest anytime soon. I called Mrs. Debbie and took off work for "family reasons," when really, I was lying on the person I knew was responsible for these two golf balls under my skully. I believed in my heart that when I saw him, it was going to be another *First 48*. It was no stopping me. I was already committed.

I'm a firm believer that we can manifest anything we focus our energy on. Man, did I think about this person all day, every day. Then, guess what happened? Satan allowed him to walk right toward me.

I was getting my car detailed when I noticed him walking from a distance. My heart began pumping through my chest. It was all or nothing. This was the moment I'd been waiting for. I reached into my glove compartment and retrieved my gun. He never saw me coming. I walked right up on him and shot him point-blank, twice. Once in the head, and once in his face. I remember standing over him, about to finish him off. I could see that he was still breathing. That's when my childhood friend snapped me out of it and pushed me back into my car, telling me to pull off. I was in total shock. I couldn't believe what I had just done. I cut my phone off and drove home in complete silence.

When I got home, I turned on the eleven o'clock news and there was no murder reported. I smoked a couple of blunts and waited up for the five o'clock morning news. Still, no homicide was reported. I turned my phone back on and saw that I had over a hundred missed messages. My friend was like, "He didn't die. He's in stable condition."

My mind began racing. I had to kill this nucca. If not, I knew for sure he was going to retaliate. I was on my way to the hospital to finish him off when my cousin called and convinced me to turn my car around. He was like, "Handle it in the streets. You pull a stunt like that… they're going to label you a terrorist."

I turned around, drove back home, and smoked two blunts to the face. I needed some rest.

I was awakened by my mother calling me, screaming in my ear that the police had her entire house surrounded, front and back.

She was like, "They said you're armed and dangerous and for you to turn yourself in."

I told my mom I would have my lawyer on top of everything, and I apologized for the inconvenience.

Later that evening, I talked to my lawyer, Michael Andrew Sacks, and he said that the victim told the police I shot him. I almost dropped my phone. Man, it's a dirty game. Just when I thought we were going to handle it in the streets like real men, he went and told the white man on me.

I knew I should've killed him, but then again, to be honest... I'm glad I didn't.

Devil In A Red Dress

I was sitting in the Norfolk City Jail, punch drunk. Not only did I have a slew of charges, but the judge also denied my bond. *Would you believe me if I told you this coward told the police that I shot and robbed him?*

My lawyer, Andrew Sacks, sat across from me and began reading the police report. It read:

"At approximately zero one hundred hours, several units responded to a shooting at the 800 block of Norview Avenue. The victim was in stable condition when police and EMS arrived on the scene. The victim suffered two bullet contusions to the face and head but was still able to communicate with authorities. The victim stated that 'Jae-Jae with the black Lexus from Young's Park' was the perpetrator.

After further investigation, our Narcotics Unit and lead investigator, Agent Lamont Vick, identified Jeremy Davis, aka Jae-Jae, a known drug dealer from the 900 block of Smith Street. His photo was picked out by the victim in a lineup. A warrant was issued, and the arrest was properly executed.

Upon arrival, our SWAT team surrounded the residence. Mr. Davis exited the house with his hands held high. He was detained and arrested without incident. A large, undisclosed amount of money was recovered, confiscated, and turned over to narcotics and federal agents. No weapons or drugs were reported from the scene."

I looked at my lawyer, disgusted. "How the hell they just gonna take all my *fucking* money and deny my bond? What part of the game is this?!"

I was already on probation in two different cities, on top of this new case. Sacks said the D.A. had offered a plea deal of **thirty years**. He told me not to worry too much and promised to get me another bond hearing ASAP.

My heart dropped.

I couldn't imagine doing half that time. I needed to get out of jail as soon as possible. I had my people reach out to Sabrina with the bad news. She came to visit me and said she'd hold off on selling the house. I asked her to sell my Lexus instead, so I could pay Andrew Sacks' expensive ass. He wasn't even taking a case without a $20,000 retainer fee. She found a buyer that week, and I sold my baby.

I refused to ask anybody else for help. A lot of family and friends had already shown their true colors when the money stopped flowing. It almost seemed like they were happy to see the champ down and out. I became the topic of everyone's tired-ass conversations.
All that talking, and not one single soul offered to help me, but I never sweated it. Somehow, I knew I would bounce back. I always did. I was born with that **dawg** in me.

Sabrina bonded me out two weeks later. She was waiting right there the moment I walked out. She was standing in her usual casual attire and sexy six-inch heels, looking thicker than ever. I could tell from our hug that she was really feeling me. The truth is that the feeling was mutual. I just didn't want to cross any boundaries. I'd always kept business with women strictly business. I learned that from experience.

She said she told the neighbors it was a mix-up, and I was released the same night. She had been staying at my house since coming back from Germany, and said things didn't work out there. So, she had to move into her new condo in three weeks. That was cool with me. I told her she could stay as long as she needed and thanked her for everything, but she was really pushing it by walking around the house with that big ol' booty.

I stayed there most evenings and worked at Genesis during the day. My Uncle Dwight looked out for me. He'd always hire me… no questions asked. Still, I had to come up with a plan. These people were talking about sentencing me to **three decades**. So, every day after work, I looked high and low for that coward-ass nucca. I wasn't going to harm him, but to see if I could persuade him with some money not to show up at trial. When I tell you dude was *M.I.A.*, missing in action. *Nobody* Uptown had seen or heard from him. I couldn't believe it. All I could do now was prepare for the fight of my life, but I needed more money to pay my dream team of lawyers.

Eric Courshener, Michael Broccoletti, and Andrew Sacks were all top-tier lawyers at the time. Broccoletti and Courshener were already repping me, and they were partners at the same law firm, but they only handled drug offenses. Sacks beat violent cases on the regular. If he couldn't beat it, he could still get your time significantly knocked down. I just kept my fingers crossed and went to work, trying to figure out a new way to get some money.

I came home one evening, and it smelled like Bob Marley and The Wailers had just smoked out the whole damn house. I was in complete shock. I never knew Sabrina smoked. I watched her walk out of the shower with her eyes bloodshot red.

"Damn! You high as giraffe thoughts, woman. I didn't even know you smoked!"

"You never asked," she said with a giggle, standing there in just a towel.

I needed to smoke now myself. My thoughts were racing in my lil' head. I rolled up and made a few phone calls. Sabrina walked back downstairs and hit the blunt, wearing those lil' booty shorts.

"Damn, you thick!" I said.

She burst out laughing again and walked into the kitchen.

She made me a cold-cut turkey and cheese hoagie with toasted bread, Lay's potato chips, and fruit punch. A straight missile. That woman could make a sandwich!

After we ate, we smoked another blunt, and I took a hot shower. Minutes later, I felt a cool breeze hit me, and guess who was standing there, naked, holding a blunt in her mouth.

Statute of Limitations

I was sitting in the crib like, *what the hell just happened?*

I was literally just banging big booty Sabrina out on my brand new raspberry sectional for the past two hours. Real spill, that was some of the best fellatio I'd had in years.

That's word.

White girls go all out to please their man... that shit was just different, but don't get it twisted, I'll take my beautiful sisters any day over a Caucasian woman. I was just wondering where we were going to take it from here. She was months away from retiring from the military, and she had started working part-time again at a popular local bar her cousin owned called *Have A Nice Day Café*. She told me she did a little bit of everything like bartending, cooking, even helping her cousin count the money at the end of the night. She said her brother had sacrificed his life savings to go half with her cousin on the club, but after a year into the business, he was tragically killed in a car accident. Her cousin had made big promises to take care of her and her mother for the rest of their lives, but he never came through like he said he would. Just a couple hundred dollars here and there, maybe covered their rent.

She said she watched him turn one club into two, and two into four. Before she knew it, dude was a multimillionaire right in front of her face, and he still hadn't made sure her mother was good. She said her brother had to be turning over in his grave, because all he ever talked about was making sure their mom was straight once the club business blew up.

She told me that she counted over a hundred thousand dollars every weekend. I was like *damn!* She went on to say that she knew from the day we met that I was about my paper. She said my cousin Monica had called and given her the real spill on me and what I was really about. She said she was attracted to my aura and had been looking forward to getting to know me, but it seemed like I was more into the house than I was into her. I let her know I was always down to make a dollar.

I definitely was! I needed a roof over my head at the time, for real.

We talked for the next hour, and she started telling me the ins and outs of the club…the exits, the security, and where all the money was kept. She said her cousin owned four clubs, but he kept all his money at that particular one until the weekend. Every Sunday, he left the club with hundreds of thousands in cash, but only took a hundred thousand at a time for security reasons. The rest was left upstairs in the floorboard under the computer desk, and it never held less than half a million.

During the weekdays, it was likely no less than three hundred thousand. I told her I needed real facts and the full layout of the club. She was with it. She told me to come through the following Saturday night. A local rapper was performing, and she knew it would be a mixed crowd, so I could peep the scene myself. I could get a feel for how the club operated.

I was like, *hell yeah!*

I called my cousin and gave him the spill. He was born trained to go and said, "Let me know the time and place. I'm there, Cuzz!"

I showed up at the club by myself that night. I stayed away from Sabrina as much as I could because I didn't want nobody catching a connection between us. We made eye contact, and she nodded to let me know who her cousin was. It was a tall, nerdy-looking white dude. I noticed he had a taser on his hip.

Dude was trippin', I thought, *He just asking for somebody to get mad.*

His security detail? All tall, slender-built men. No Deebo-looking goons except for the obese one working the front door. I noticed three exits, and I peeped the upstairs office near the fourth. I kept boppin' my head to the music and sippin' my water, but in my head I was calculating and strategizing my next move.

I called Cuzzo back and asked if he was ready. I told him *tonight's the night.* We weren't going to strike 'til five in the morning because that's when the owner usually left out the back door. He was hyped, and asked, "Can my boy come too? He thorough and trained to go. He can hold the door for a few dollars." He sounded convincing. Somehow, I let him talk me into it, even though I wasn't feeling dude.

We pulled up around 4 AM… just in time to scope out the scene. Everything looked normal. Sabrina texted me from her burner, saying dude would be leaving in less than two minutes and that he had one other person with him, but neither one had a gun.

I texted back,

You sure?

'Cause if that's true, this was going to be one of the easiest licks of the century.

She replied, saying the one security guard with the gun was upstairs with the safe. I gave my cousin the game plan, and we moved like somebody stole our money. As soon as the back door opened, Cuzzo put the gun to the dude's head and pushed him back inside. We told the other man to get on the ground. We duct-taped his legs and feet, then headed for the steps… right where we knew the bankroll was. We made the owner yell up to the security guard to put his gun down and come out with his hands up!

Cuzzo duct-taped him, too. We didn't go straight for the floorboard 'cause if we did, they'd know it was an inside job. We had thirty seconds to ransack the office first, then hit the stash.

Man, when I tell you I had never seen so much cash in my life.

We had ***four trash bags*** full.

Cuzzo

Dre held the door down until we exited and made it to the truck. That gave me enough time to throw two bags into the trunk. Then, I placed the other two in the back seat of the SUV. Dre had no idea the money bags in the trunk even existed.

We drove the speed limit for the next thirty minutes until we finally arrived at a motel on the other side of the city. I wanted to separate myself as far as possible from the crime scene. On the ride there, I couldn't stop replaying the heist over in my head. I was just hoping we didn't slip up or make any foolish mistakes. We were all masked up, so there was no way they could've recognized us. We had on gloves, so no fingerprints were left behind, and our vehicle was an all-black SUV with dark tints and no license plate. It's hundreds… if not thousands… of black trucks driving around in the seven cities.

We finally pulled into the motel. I was glad to see that it was laid-back and there weren't a lot of people walking around or standing on the banisters being nosey. I didn't want to look suspect taking trash bags out of the truck. The most important thing was that nobody was killed or hurt in the process. You can't replace a life, but you can always replace money.

After we checked in, we poured both bags of money onto the bed and started counting and stacking it into thousand-dollar piles. After about an hour and a half, it totaled up to a hundred and fifty-eight thousand. I paid Dre fifty thousand and told Cuzzo I was gonna get him straight later because we still had to split the rest three ways.

We dropped Dre off at his girlfriend's house, but before he exited, I respectfully asked him to chill for at least a week with the spending. The police were going to be looking for anybody throwing around large amounts of money too fast. I said that because I overheard him telling Cuzzo he was going to buy an Acura Legend. He pounded me up and assured me he would wait it out for two weeks. By the time I got home, it was almost seven in the morning. Me Cuzzo and I, sat in my living room and counted the other two bags for the next two and a half hours. Altogether, it totaled $500,158!

We looked at each other like*, Damn!!! We actually hit a lick for half a ticket.*

I paid Cuzzo eighty grand. That left me with four hundred and twenty thousand dollars. I couldn't believe it. I still had one more person to pay, so I split it evenly down the middle with Sabrina. She arrived home around ten-thirty, excited. She said she broke her burner phone and flushed it as soon as she got off the phone with me. She went on to say the police didn't even know what kind of vehicle we drove away in. She said they asked a lot of questions, but they never suspected any of the club workers had anything to do with it.

She said she got nervous when they asked her cousin, "How did the suspects know you had someone upstairs guarding the safe in the floor? You said the suspects told you to yell for your security to come out, right?"

His only response was, "I always have security upstairs…everybody knows that."

Then, they interviewed her, and instantly, she put on her frightened white woman Karen face and voice. The detective asked her where she was during the robbery, and she replied that she hid in the stock room. She had to think quickly, because if she said she was anywhere else, they would've asked why she didn't call the police or try to escape. They left and told her it was an ongoing investigation, and if she came up with any new leads, to give them a call. Her cousin wasn't as upset as she expected. He just said he had to double up on security and add more cameras outside. He didn't even know how much money was taken because it was unaccounted for that night. She said that was all the questions they asked.

After she left, she headed straight home. She gave me a big hug and kiss. I walked over, retrieved her cut from the closet, and poured it on the bed. When I told her it was all hers, she almost fainted. We smoked a couple of blunts and drank champagne, celebrating another victory for the rest of the day.

Six months later, I pulled up on the scene in a newer model Lexus 430. Everyone was looking crazy, like my bounce back wasn't official. I even had a diamond necklace, watch, and bracelet. I had to get my shit off, because so many people had turned their backs and left me for dead. Now, I was back, and looking like I'd just come off a fifty-city tour. I was bankroll fresh, and I knew everyone around me knew it, but things were different now. I didn't move the same, and I didn't embrace a lot of friends or family. They counted the champ out, but they should've known better.

I was rich now. The past six months I'd been flipping cocaine and selling exotic pounds of weed consistently. I moved differently. I even had my young shooters from Chesapeake rolling with me. I made sure they had that go-getter mentality and weren't hardheaded. They all had their driver's licenses, and I groomed them into official hustlers. At one time, I purchased five cars from the auction for a light twenty grand, and everywhere I went, I showed up six cars deep. When I pulled off, they did too.

My OG Skeeno pulled me to the side and schooled me. He said, "I see you doing your thing, but you don't want the people to hit you with a RICO charge."

At that time, I was clueless. I was like, "What the hell is that, Unk?"

That's when he said, "It's what you're doing. Running an organized drug operation. It's clear as day, and they don't come with anything less than a life sentence."

That was my OG, and I knew everything he told me was out of love. There's just no wins in this shit. I was just trying to get some money and protect myself while doing it.

I decided at that moment... I wasn't ever going to hustle again...

Modern Day Plantation...

I entered into a world that was designed for me to self-destruct... physically, mentally, and spiritually. A modern-day slave plantation that was filled with violent gang activity, robberies, stabbings, homosexuality, rapes, and people dying daily from fentanyl overdoses. A place divided by race. The Blacks walked, ate, and worked out together. So did the Aryan Nation and the Spanish MS-13 gangs.

It was a world where they fed you non-nutritional food and paid you only thirty-five cents an hour. All you could afford were their high-sodium products like noodles, cookies, and honey buns off the overpriced commissary list. Just like seventy-five percent of the population, you'd eventually become prediabetic or full-blown diabetic. That's when their second phase begins. They start pumping you with all sorts of pills, medications, and injections. It's all part of their elaborate plan to slowly destroy the Black man.

What person do you know in their right mind could survive in a place like this?

Exactly.

That's why I found my own answer. It came the minute I decided to dedicate my energy to the universal law of attraction. Deep down, down, I always knew, deep down, that there was a Creator, but man has manipulated everything he's touched, especially religion. I've been around all kinds of religions, and none of them brought me peace of mind, solace, love, or the kind of happiness I've found through the law of attraction. It's not a religion... it's energy!

I believe a lot of religious folks just want to hand their problems over to God and go on with their day. They continue to sin, over and over, just to pray it away later. Nobody wants to take accountability for their *own* ways, thoughts, and actions.

Did you know that slave masters used to rape and sodomize our ancestors throughout the night? When morning came, they'd ask if they had a ,"Good Ole Moaning!"

That's why I will never say that again. When you know better, you do better.

It's *Grand Rising*... to the sun, moon, and stars...to the Universe!

After they raped our great-great-grandmothers, they sent them to church with their wives to worship the same "God."

Did you know that in the Old Testament, it actually says that a slave should obey their master? That our great-grandmothers taught that same logic to our grandmothers, who taught it to our mothers, who taught it to us, in turn.

Damn.

Our African ancestors are turning in their graves. They didn't even know who Jesus Christ was.

Our ancestors were spiritual people. They set fires and danced around them in praise while giving thanks to the sun, the moon, the stars, and of course, the universe. Imhotep was a deity who performed the same miracles as Jesus, healing the sick and curing disease, long before Jesus ever existed. He even traveled with outlaws, just like Jesus... but you've probably never heard of him, huh?

That's because the white man stole the original scrolls and burned them. Then, they rewrote history. They tricked us…and are still tricking us with their 70-inch *"tel-LIE-visions"* that you keep catching on sale every Black Friday. They're projecting lies and false narratives into our homes and trapping our people in a matrix of deceit. Every Black person who hasn't experienced the awakening is still a slave.

That's just facts.

The white man had four hundred years to come up with these master plans and they said it would take another four hundred years for us to figure it out. I'm grateful to the universe for revealing the truth. I was able to reset my thinking, open my third eye, and see that everything I had believed my entire life was a lie.

However, I learned that I could control and manifest my own destiny.

Through the power of the law of attraction, I've reached the highest version of myself. I treated prison like college. I read and studied everything from self-help manuals to financial freedom books to stock market guides to money management to banking. I earned certificates in several trades such as plumbing, electrical work, carpentry, and brick masonry. I became a master barber, an artist, and a **best-selling author** with books in Barnes & Noble, Walmart, Target, and Amazon. I launched my own publishing company, **Uptown Classic Publications**. My credit score?...Over 700, and still climbing.

I did all this right under their noses and on *their* plantation.

A place meant to break me down.

I may have lost the battle in the streets, but I *won the war* on their plantation.

And guess what?

It feels amazing.

I refused to eat their garbage. I ate beans, fruits, and vegetables only. I became the best version of myself. If you ask me whether I'd do it all again... if I'd rewind time and undo it... I honestly wouldn't. There's no amount of money or material items that compares to the feeling of being *woke* and *in control* of your own destiny.

To the OG who was in the bullpen, I appreciate your advice to sign that plea deal. You saved my life, and I'll never forget you. When I first got to prison, I hated that I listened to you. Then, I started meeting men with less serious charges doing *way* more time than I.

The end of this journey is near.

It's been challenging...mentally, physically, and spiritually.

But I won.

I won because I found my identity... and fulfilled my purpose in life!

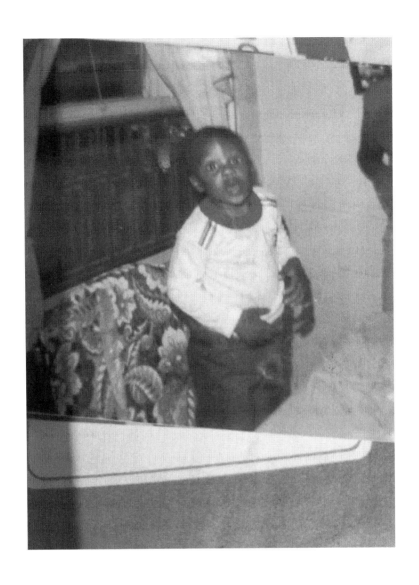

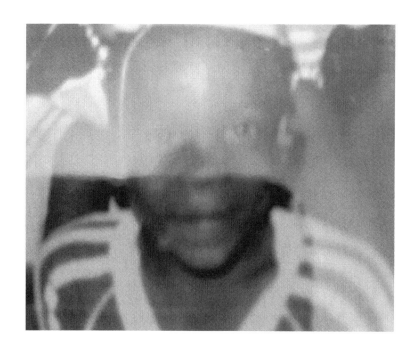

Made in the USA
Columbia, SC
14 July 2025